PROV
SAINT
NICK

ECHO GRAYCE

Beautiful Misfits Press

BeautifulMisfitsPress@gmail.com

Publisher's Note: This is a work of fiction. All names, characters, locations, and incidents are products of the author's imagination. Locales and public names are sometimes used for atmospheric purposes. Any resemblance to actual persons, things, living or dead, or to businesses, companies, events, institutions, or locales is entirely coincidental.

Edited By: Editing by Kimberly Dawn

Cover Design: Wildheart Graphics

Cover Image: Sarah Kil Creative Studio

PROVOKING SAINT NICK / Echo Grayce. — 1st ed.

Find the people who don't mind you being a little bit broken.

The ones who say...
"I'll hold your broken pieces with you while you figure out how to put them back together again."

Brooke Montgomery...
this one's for you.

I
NICK

G od grant me the serenity to not choke the wildcard of rich bitches.

Charlie fucking McAllister.

My best friend's little sister. Tormentor extraordinaire. Star of my every trauma as a teenager.

Oh, the irony of the youngest daughter of the richest family in Bar Harbor standing with her jean-clad hip propped against the Eat the Rich sticker. The pithy act of defiance clung crookedly to the back of a rusted Jeep Wrangler.

Yeah, that was on brand for the little demon.

I bet Mommy and Daddy just loved that.

It was one week. I could handle her for one week.

When we were kids, she jacked my chili with pickling spices and when I gagged, she saved me by handing me a tomato juice laced with ghost pepper sauce.

When I broke my arm junior year and her mother insisted she help me pack for a trip to Boston, she cut the crotch out of every pair of underwear, shorts, and pants she packed in my duffel.

I flexed my fingers on the wheel, my one small show

3

of anxiety because there was no way she didn't notice me pulling in and the longer I sat here, the more ideas she'd get.

If I just kept her away from my food and my suitcase, I might just make it out of this unscathed.

Only, everything about her narrowed eyes and the smirk tilting those full lips at the corners told me she was waiting for me, and she was up to something.

I grabbed my cell and shot off a text to Chance. This was my last rant until I got pushed through the annual McAllister/McAdams Christmas ski week.

For thirty years, on the week of Christmas, our families inconvenienced all of us at the worst possible time by summoning our presence. This was the third year in a row Chance missed, the military making it hard as hell for him to be home. I got it… but I didn't have to be happy about it.

ME

You're a real boner for not being here this week.

CHANCE

Turned to shit already, huh?

ME

Your sister is here.

CHANCE

You'll have to be more specific. I have two.

ME

Charlie, you asshole.

CHANCE

BAHAHAHAHAHAHAHAHA… good luck!

ME

Fuck you. May you catch your fucking dick in your zipper.

CHANCE

Dude, don't joke about that shit.

ME

Who's joking?

CHANCE

You'll be fine. Charlie's fun.

ME

If you're a sadist.

CHANCE

Actually, if you're a masochist. She'd be the sadist.

ME

Jesus, you think just like her.

CHANCE

You're not wrong, but you love me anyway.

ME

Yeah, well, just don't expect roses on Valentine's Day.

CHANCE

Baby, you never buy me flowers anymore.

ME

Cute.

CHANCE

You'll have fun. Just don't fuck her.

I froze with my thumb hovering over the keyboard. Not going to lie, if it didn't promise pain, definite stalking, and starring in a future episode of *Snapped*... nah, not even then.

ME

...

CHANCE

Confirm asshole. No fucking my baby sister.

Huh, seemed like he was getting mad.

ME

...

CHANCE

Listen, fucker... DO. NOT. FUCK. MY. SISTER.

Definitely mad. So, there was an upside this weekend. No peace for me, but then none for him either.

ME

...

CHANCE

When I get my hands—

I didn't bother reading the rest of his message and instead whipped out the finale with a smile on my face.

ME

Now that you're just as miserable, peace out. And guy, really? I know the code. Besides, if I were planning to fuck one of your sisters, it would be Eve.

CHANCE

I don't like how you dropped her name like you had it in your head, ready to go.

ME

Later, dude.

I climbed out of my SUV, ignored the demon spawn, and circled around to the hatch to grab my bag. I'd hold on to it until I was in my room. Preferably on the opposite side of the resort.

She propped her bag against my back tire and leaned on my car. "We need to talk."

"No, we don't."

"You're not curious who I spotted when I got here then? Okay." She settled her sunglasses on the bridge of her nose and shrugged. "I thought you'd want a warning, but—"

I hitched my bag over my shoulder, shut the hatch, and crossed my arms. "Fine, who did you see, Charlotte?"

"Gross, don't call me that." She shivered and looked just like her mother when Chance and I tracked across her brand-new white tile foyer during her annual New Year's party. The first and last party she'd allowed us to invite our friends to. Somehow, I didn't think Charlie would appreciate the comparison.

Instead, I tucked it away in my arsenal for later.

"It's your name."

Her lips flattened into a hard line. "It's on my birth certificate. That doesn't make it my name, Nicholas."

I grinned as I tossed my keys in the air and caught them easily. "Nice try, but my name doesn't bother me."

She raised her chin with smug delight. "But it bothers you when I call you Saint N—"

"Don't start that shit, Charlie." Irritation spiked my blood, and I shoved my fingers through my hair to keep from strangling her.

She'd gotten it in her twisted little head years ago that I was some sort of paragon of virtue. I wasn't. I just wasn't obvious about my recreational activities.

"Saint Nick is so dreamy. He's so smart."

Chance said not to fuck her. He didn't say I couldn't strangle her.

A rogue image flashed in my mind of my hand curled around her throat, her eyes glazed over… Jesus, okay, so 'fuck' and 'strangle' were clearly two verbs that didn't belong anywhere near each other in my head.

This was all Chance's fault. He's the one who'd brought up fucking her and inadvertently planted some sort of subliminal spank bank inspiration in my psyche.

The prick.

"The star player on every team. Le sigh. When he walks by, I just can't help but go tits up, ready for Saint Nick to—"

"Your parents should have spanked you." I pinched the bridge of my nose and squinted at the sudden pain throbbing in my skull.

"Aww, picturing me getting spanked. That's not very virtuous, Saint Nick."

Gritting my teeth, I took a step toward her. A menacing step. Every bit of frustration from the past week at my job colliding with the mouthy pain in the ass standing before me.

The snarl that rose from my throat had her hands up and surrendering… well, as much as Charlie surrendered to anything.

"Okay, easy… Don't need to tarnish the halo or anything. I just thought you might want to know that your parents arrived with your favorite blond parasite."

"You're lying."

She crossed her arms and casually leaned against my car. "Nope, pretty boy. She looked straight out of Saks and ready to pin you under her lethal-looking Jimmy Choo until you agree to put a ring on it."

"I'd rather eat dirt."

"That's what I thought, so I figured I'd do you a favor so you can avoid that fate."

"A deal with the Devil sounds like better odds."

One week with Mariah Quinn, as a favor to my mother, and I hadn't shaken her since. A cool and collected classy package on the outside, but pure venom pumped with cruel glee in her frigid heart.

She had zero chance at ever being anything to me. If she sank that heel into my chest, I'd bleed out before I'd give in to a life of poison.

Charlie branded me a saint, but I wasn't. I just valued kindness and respect. If you were in my circle, I gave it freely. Everyone I met was in until they gave me a reason to push them out.

She reached for her bag with a single shoulder shrug. "Okay. Well, good luck with Mariah. I'll see you at the lodge. I'll be the one with the popcorn."

A soul-sucking week of tactical maneuvers with Charlie waiting in the wings to pile on the snark loomed before me. I choked back the bitterness of surrender and reached out to grasp her arm. "Wait. What are you thinking?"

She glanced up at me, her eyes sparkling with victory. "All we have to do is show up together and you won't have to worry about fending off the ice queen."

"We are showing up together." I had to be out of my mind to even consider this. Our families were intertwined like a strand of DNA. Our mothers had successfully remained best friends for over forty years. This plan meant a lifetime of our families reminding us we were an item once.

She rolled her eyes. "I mean together. As in, a couple."

"A couple of what?"

One golden brown eyebrow arched. "Jesus Nick. A

couple. Like tab A in slot B… a couple," she said while poking her teal-tipped index finger through the ring she made with her other finger and thumb. "Tell me you haven't had that dick on such tight lockdown it doesn't even know what that is anymore."

"You want to be my girlfriend?"

She let out a flippant laugh followed by a snort. "God, no. You could not handle me. But for the week… we could pretend. If done right, we'll have a good time on the slopes instead of spending the whole time dodging our mothers—"

"Ah, I get it."

"Good, because I was worried I needed to draw you a picture."

Her shoulders relaxed, a sure tell this arrangement was not from the kindness of her heart, but for her own benefit.

Gotcha, little demon. I slid my hands in my pockets and rocked back on my heels. "Your mom brought someone for you too, didn't she?"

"What—no," she scoffed, the telltale sound of bullshit.

I grinned. "Liar."

"I don't l—"

"Careful, you're about to tell one right now." I curled my fingers under the strap of the duffel and slid it from her arm. "Who'd she bring?"

"Listen—"

"Who did she bring, Charlie?" I settled her bag over my shoulder.

Her gaze darted away and when she finally turned back, a grimace twisted her usually sassy mouth. "Daniel Sloan."

My gaze snapped to hers where I caught a riot of emotions flitting through her piercing gray eyes. "He's your—"

"Ex. Yeah. Which is even worse. Apparently, I'm so repugnant she can't peddle me to a new guy, so she has to convince the old guy to take me back."

"Ouch." Mrs. McAllister had just moved a fraction toward the outer edge of my circle with that move.

Charlie shifted on her feet and chewed her lip. "Do we have a deal or not?"

Her mischievous energy dimmed with her admission and show of nerves. I couldn't put my finger on why, but I didn't like it.

"Deal," I said, offering my hand to shake on it.

She shot me a suspicious glance. "Really? You're not fucking with me, right?"

"According to you, I'm not that interesting." I smiled and winked, letting her know we're good. Something to get us back on solid Charlie and Nick ground where she was the scheming jester devising new ways to make me her fool.

Because as much as the jester was a pain in my ass, wounded Charlie sparked something in me I didn't recognize. Something I didn't care to examine. "Take my hand, Charlie."

Her hand slid into mine and something shifted. Impossibly soft skin settled against my palm and her warm, tight grip had the hair along my neck prickling. Somewhere inside me alarm bells went off.

My best friend's warning about his little sister burned in my pocket with my cell.

This week was about to punch me right in the dick.

2
Charlie

I never thought for a second Saint Nick would agree to my proposition. I mean, yes, he's saint-worthy. So freaking squeaky clean I had the unshakable urge to spin my tires in a pile of mud and coat him from head to toe with unexpected fuckery.

Despite his golden boy ways, he'd never once extended his saintly gestures to me.

Not that I'd earned them. I'd spent a lifetime torturing him, doing anything and everything to get a rise out of him. Just aching to see one perfect strand of hair slide out of place. Just once.

He was just so inherently… good. Everything he touched turned to success. Nothing handed to him, just a natural ability to try something and in no time at all, excel at it.

Nick approached everything with unflappable patience and dedication, soon after he slid effortlessly into mastery.

No strutting or bragging.

His accidental perfection was unsettling.

Which meant he was the absolute perfect solution to

thwart my mother and whatever she had up her sleeve with Daniel.

If he didn't drive me out of my mind before then.

Sunshine danced over his skin, glinting on the facial hair he'd let grow in. Even the awkward stage between sexy scruff and neat beard was perfect.

He was completely oblivious to it. And wasn't that a punch in the tit? He was simply indifferent to his benevolence.

My proximity to Nick always seemed to highlight my inadequacies. Or so I thought. But perhaps proximity was the key. After all, if they believed I managed to snag him, that had to be points in my favor, right?

Well, feigned proximity. Whatever got us through the weekend. The bare minimum of polite PDA when we were in the company of our families and that was it.

I certainly didn't expect to earn me favorite status. Chance had that position locked tight by being selfless and going into the Army. Then when he had the opportunity to get out, he went career. Welp, there was no way in hell for me to compete with that.

And Eve, well, she worked in a predominantly male field as a carpenter and wouldn't be caught dead at one of our parents' dinner parties, rubbing elbows with our parents' friends, our dad's business associates, or God forbid, fending off some of the prospects our mother marched her way. No one even dared hint at her putting on a designer dress. They probably feared her coming at them with a nail gun. But she got a pass because she spent so much time sick as a kid.

So that left me. The one who couldn't be set up, steered in their direction, or settle down.

The one who actually loved her job as a massage therapist, a career choice my mother told me more than once was beneath a McAllister.

Basically, I was the fuck up.

Nick could be my arm candy… and my mom adored him, so it was a win-win. She'd be planning our babies before our heads hit the pillow tonight.

Our boots clicked over the damp asphalt as we made our way to the resort to meet our families and check-in. We had maybe five minutes before we jumped under the microscope of two nosy mothers.

"Okay, so we need some rules."

His lips quirked. "I'm pretty sure only one of us needs rules. Lots of rules."

"Funny." I adjusted my garment bag on my shoulder. "If you plan to sell yourself as my boyfriend, especially to our mothers, you'll have to treat me like I'm not Nair headed straight for your balls."

His head swung to mine, and he pierced me with a wary stare. "Is that a move from your playbook I haven't encountered yet?"

"Yet, but we're young. There's still time." I patted his shoulder and laughed at his horrified expression.

His assessing gaze raked over me, and his mouth turned down at the corners. "Maybe I just have a healthy fear your vagina has teeth and I'm not dumb enough to go anywhere near that nightmare."

"Well, the joke's on you… I have a fabulous vagina. Very responsive."

"Your parents should have grounded you more," he muttered next to me.

Choosing to ignore his surly disposition at the mere mention of my lady bits, I continued. "Besides, there's nothing healthy about you fearing any vagina. Move that to the top of the list to tackle with your therapist. Lucky for us, you won't have to get near my big, scary vagina to make it through the week. Neither of our parents will expect PDA if I'm dating you—"

He snorted. "Why does that feel like a dig?"

The frigid air chugged in and out of my lungs, leaving a biting sting with every breath. Cars rolled through the north entrance and lined up, waiting to unload. The resort gleamed as it did early in the season, with their vast revamping efforts from during the offseason on full display.

"Not a dig, just truth. You're not flashy, pretty boy. But that works for us. We can go through this whole week with you doing nothing more than pulling out my chair and brushing your hand over my lower back when you guide me into a room. Oooh," I said with a snap of my fingers. "And make a show of holding my hand at some point and our parents will be neck deep in planning our wedding and the littles to follow."

He skidded to a stop. "Littles?"

I grabbed his hand and tugged him back to my side. "Kids."

"Jesus."

"Jesus was a nice guy and all, but he can't help you. Don't worry. I've got your back."

"Terrifying," he muttered.

"Isn't it? Anyway, just treat me like I'm human. I'll put a hold on the Nair, and in a week, we'll both have our freedom. Actually, less than a week when you think about it. Five days. We can handle five days. And no worrying about teeth… you won't be going near either set." Laughter bubbled up in my throat, releasing some of the tension coiled in my gut.

"Christ."

"Ah, ah, no swearing, Saint Nick."

"And it's six days. Five nights, but six whole days."

I yanked open the door for him, patted him on the shoulder, and gave him a little shove since it looked like his feet might refuse to take another step. The blood had completely drained from his face. "Get your shit together… it's showtime."

3
Charlie

A gust of warm air carrying a hint of cinnamon and chocolate washed over us the minute we stepped through the doors, reminding me of a happy childhood here. When I spent most of my time with the boys and no one judged me for it.

The main room of the lodge where families checked in opened into a two-story massive room with knotted pine walls, tall windows facing the slopes, and dueling fireplaces on each end, both with stonework shooting straight up to the ceiling.

Cozy seating areas arranged in clusters of coordinating warm creams, blush, rose, and camel shades dotted the room, most already occupied by families and kids.

So many kids.

"Does it seem busier to you this year?"

"They added two black diamond trails and a new quad. It's busier." His voice rumbled next to my ear, catching me by surprise.

"Super."

Garlands draped from corner to corner of every

21

window, giving the room an underlying scent of the fresh, crisp scent of pine. Dueling arrangements of three interlocking wreaths, each at least four feet tall, hung high on the stone-face chimneys over the twin burning fireplaces. Golden bows gleamed in the rays of the sun breaking through the clouds and streaming through the expansive skylights.

And none of it was nearly as stunning as the massive tree in the corner wrapped in a generous swath of white lights. Red suede bows adorned the tips of the branches and in between, delicate scalloped-edged angels with pleated skirts dangled from golden thread, a Christmas wish written on every single one.

And despite the kind of money everyone here had, so many of those wishes would go unanswered.

I managed to put away five thousand dollars to put toward them, and while I felt good about it, I hated that I couldn't do more.

Even more than that, I hated that my mother wouldn't bother grabbing a single one.

"There you are!" My mother feigned excitement at seeing me. Not because I was her daughter and she loved me, but no doubt because she thought she had the upper hand with Daniel firmly in her back pocket. I'm sure she thought she held on to this wonderful secret that would make me so grateful I'd act like a true McAllister for the first time.

News flash—I was a Charlie. I was going to act like a Charlie.

Which meant Daniel didn't have a chance. He never

should have had a shot even if I acted like a typical McAllister, but then that was the whole crux of the problem.

I tried. I really did. There was a time I wore dresses, hung out with the "right" kids, and made sure I got straight A's. And at the end of the day, none of it mattered. Eventually my need to stand up for myself would come out in a rush of scathing words and it would erase everything I'd done to earn her pride.

Well, silence had never been my style. Not really. I could bite my tongue for a limited amount of time before someone inevitably flipped the switch and activated my smart mouth. If there wasn't a way to contain it entirely, why bother trying to contain it at all?

Charlie logic. You're welcome.

She draped her arms daintily around my shoulders and bathed me in a cloud of Chanel No. 5. while giving me a quick air-kiss next to my cheek.

For a moment, I considered wrapping my arms around her the way I used to. A real hug like when I was a kid, before I realized it was possible to have the physical presence of two parents yet feel like an orphan.

"You're looking lovely, dear. A little puffy, but we've got a few days to work on that."

She whispered the barbs in a way no one else would hear them, but with a few sips of wine, and a group of people to cover her snide remarks with laughs, she'd get bolder. They'd become more frequent in the past few years as I pulled further away from the family and turned more and more into a person she just didn't understand.

One she had no hope of controlling.

Normally, I'd say something; after all, I'm not going to make it easy for her to throw digs my way. If she wanted to go there, she'd have to work for it by taking a few grenades of her own. But this time I had Saint Nick on my side, so maybe I could let it roll off until the buzz of our "new relationship" gave her a dopamine hit strong enough it knocked the subtle and not-so-subtle digs clean out of her.

I will not kill her. I will not kill her. I will not kill her. "Gee, looking forward to it."

Her eyes narrowed ever so slightly. "Don't be smart, dear. It's unbecoming of a young lady."

"Too bad you didn't raise one."

Her mouth pinched with disapproval before she plastered on a glowing smile for Nick.

"Nicholas, sweetheart, it's so good to see you." She took his hands in her own and beamed up at him. "Aren't you just as handsome as ever."

Fuck yeah, this was going to work wonders on the stick up her ass.

He leaned in, towering over us both by at least a foot, and kissed my mother on the cheek. "You look just gorgeous, Mrs. McAllister. I love the new haircut."

See? Smooth fucker. He did everything with ease and was just naturally good at all the things. He hadn't seen her in months. And now he was the new hairstyle spotter? The shit.

And they weren't just words. The sleek bob was new and until he mentioned it, I hadn't noticed.

I wanted to be mad, but he made eye contact with me over her shoulder and winked. For a second, the sting from her insult faded.

We were in this together. At least for the next five days—oh, excuse me, five nights and six days. I bet if I asked him, he'd know the predetermined length of our fake relationship in hours and minutes. He was a numbers guy after all.

"Nicholas! Just look at you." Mrs. McAdams swooped in and curled into Nick's chest. Mothers and sons. They were so weird.

I wouldn't call Nick a mama's boy. I remembered a few decent meals he cooked on the grill, and I'd seen him handle laundry so it wasn't like he was waiting for someone to take care of him.

But moms… they just loved doting on their little boys. My mother did it with Chance while Eve and I navigated minefields. And I'd definitely seen Mrs. McAdams do it with Nick over the course of our lives.

I rolled my eyes and at about the point my gaze reached two o'clock, my eyes locked on the asshat from hell—a total waste of perfectly good air, Daniel Sloan.

Daniel's expression slid from blasé to smug satisfaction, like he was such a fucking catch and how lucky was I that he'd shower me with his attention, especially on the single biggest holiday of the year.

Santa and his fucking lumps of coal.

And from the cocky determination on his face, the

man whore had probably rewritten our history and cast himself as some sort of paragon of virtue. The selfless savior who swooped in to make the McAllister fuckup look good. The problem with Daniel, when he set up a lie, he ran it through his head so many times he started to believe it himself. Going toe to toe with him and battling it out was a complete waste of energy and would only result in tearing your hair out in frustration.

I loved a good battle, but Daniel had never been worth it. He'd been a walking red flag from day one. He hated animals, thought kids should be seen and not heard, and treated the doorman, a charming, stooped man of almost eighty named Mr. Barnes, like absolute shit.

I low-key hoped Mr. Barnes took the opportunity to shove Daniel in front of a bus one morning.

Next to him, Mariah bit down on her bottom lip delicately because no doubt she didn't want to ding her lipstick while still conveying that come-hither energy— but really, all I got from the vibe she was sending was… *Get me, hot stuff. I have no boobs, no ass, but hey, anything from a designer hanger looks fucking phenomenal on me because I'm shaped like, well, a wire fucking hanger.*

But what really stood out was how… familiar they seemed with one another. Not a sex level—I mean, Daniel would totally fuck her; he'd fuck practically anything that moved, but Mariah? Despite hating everything about her and what she stood for, I had a hard time picturing her going there. Mariah may be calculating and mean to the core, but she wasn't stupid. She definitely wasn't desperate.

Not that I was either, but—never mind. He was an error in judgment. One of many in my life.

My mom's voice cut through my thoughts, the pitch pleasant to most, but shrill to me. "How funny you two arriving at the same time." She rested a hand on Nick's forearm and glanced between us. "We have a surprise for—"

Oh God… here it comes.

And with it, my chill fled.

"We came together," I blurted.

Two perfectly coifed blond hairdos swung in my direction.

No longer snuggled against Nick's chest, Mrs. McAdams blinked, an expression I didn't recognize settling into her gaze. "Together?" she asked, peering up at him, dismissing me entirely.

Ouch.

My mom glanced back and forth between us. "You two? But why?"

Nick's gaze eyes flicked in Mariah and Daniel's direction, like a signal just between the two of us. A sort of rudimentary fake dating way of communicating or something. A little on-the-job training.

Sink or swim, bitches.

"Because…" Nick let his mom go, took a step back from her and toward me. Why that was so fucking hot, I refused to examine. Reaching for me, he slid his hand into mine—there was that zing again; I needed to

Google how to stop that shit stat—and tugged me toward him. He spun me until we both faced our mothers with my back pressed against his chest and his free hand sliding over my stomach possessively. "Charlie's my girlfriend."

Smooth fucker.

God, he was warm. And hard. Muscled. Not hard hard. I'm pretty sure he'd consider chopping his own dick off before letting it get hard for me.

And why the hell was he holding me so tight? Like I belonged to him. I mean, I guess I did. Kinda. For fakesies and shit. But really, did he need to hold me that tight? Where my ass nestled right into his—actually, while I'm here… I wiggled, settling against him tighter.

The pads of his fingers dug into my skin. A barely perceptible growl rumbled from his chest against my back.

I tilted my head and smiled up at him, the absolute picture of adoration and love—and innocence.

It would totally be out of character—and let's face it, impossible—to give up fucking with him, so until we could go back to the way things were, this would have to keep me satisfied.

And him very dissatisfied.

Our mothers' expressions were worlds apart. My mom was absolutely ecstatic, judging by her huge smile. The smile she always strived to avoid because of lines and shit. Apparently, my managing to snag Nick warranted the risk of adding to the years that threatened to march across her face the minute she gave up chemical peels, exotic skin regimens, and Botox.

Mrs. McAdams on the other hand… Her lips puckered in the slightest hint of disapproval, and she aimed some serious side-eye at my mom.

I guess that told me where I stood.

Daniel and Mariah sidled up, both looking us over. Daniel glowered at Nick's hand on my stomach. Mariah wore a more feral version of Mrs. McAdams' expression, also one hundred percent aimed at me.

Nick smiled next to me, his bearded cheek brushing mine, oblivious to the battle lines forming between two best friends.

"This is actually perfect," my mother gushed. "There was a problem with the rooms. We were going to be one short, but since you two can room together, I can let the desk know we're all set."

4
NICK

"Rooming together was not part of the deal," I growled down at the little demon as we headed to the private dining room. Normally, we'd all head up to our rooms to unpack before we met for cocktails at six. By six thirty, we'd head to our dinner reservation, but the influx of people staying for the week changed everything.

The concierge had our bags, we had no clue what to expect from our shared room, and the settling in I looked forward to, now wouldn't happen until after dinner. A time I used to relish spending in the lodge bar with Chance.

He'd pay for abandoning me... again. Yes, it wasn't his fault, but at the moment, I couldn't care less.

I thought I could do this. Minimal touching. Polite. Act like I actually liked her. Limited displays of affection, but there was no warm-up, no time-outs, no water breaks.

By flipping the routine, I was in this... all the way in it for the next several hours. I didn't have time for the freak-out I so desperately needed after the way I fought my body's reaction to her.

My head may not be all in on this ruse, but my dick slapped his thigh and jumped on the horse with a rowdy yeehaw like he was about to live his best life.

The dipshit and I were going to have a long talk about whatever the hell kind of brain damage he'd suffered between rolling in the parking lot and checking into the hotel that suddenly had him wanting to dive all the way into this fake relationship.

Daniel's condescending gaze traveling the length of Charlie's body only made it worse. Somewhere in the depths of my brain, my psyche whispered words I failed to realize could activate possessiveness in me.

He's had her.

Why the hell did that bother me so much? Other than the obvious, she was too good for him. Anyone could see that, couldn't they?

But her mother didn't.

Fuck.

Why could I see it?

She shot an elbow into my ribs. "Well, it's not like I planned it to be stuck in a hotel room with you, hotshot. And you're welcome, by the way. My presence adds a level of protection for you, because Queen Succubus up there had plans for you. Sinister plans."

They couldn't be worse than the very round, soft, way-too-fuckable ass Charlie just ground on my dick in the lobby. Thankfully, she'd slipped from my grip before she discovered my very real, raging hard-on growing against her. It took everything to fight my instinct to grind against her, especially when Daniel's gaze met mine in challenge.

Bring it, you shithead. You'll lose.

Lines blurred. The unwelcome stirring of trouble swirled in my gut and hadn't stopped two-stepping on my peace of mind since.

Don't fuck my baby sister…

Cool, guy. Got you.

But who would keep her from fucking me?

Only in every single way but the one involving a spine-tingling orgasm for me. Not that I wanted her. My dick seemed to, but that was just chemistry, biology, animal instinct—whatever. He didn't run this shit. I did.

Chance would not get out of this without suffering. I'd come up with a way to fuck with him even half a world away.

"Your mother was chilly."

I blinked down at her, at the quiet hesitation in her voice, the words taking a minute to process because until today, I'd never once heard Charlie anything other than confident, brash, and larger than life. This was the second hint of vulnerability in less than an hour, throwing one more unknown into our new dynamic.

The new dynamic that messed with my regimented life in every single way.

"What? No, she wasn't."

She stopped short and whipped around with her cool glare in place. "Really? Who got the better end of this deal?" she said with a snort. "My mom got you, and your mom…"

I took a step toward her and told myself I did it to keep this conversation from blocking the entire hallway. When really, I didn't want to leave her any way to escape. Reaching behind her, I clasped the end of that wavy ponytail and gave it a tug, tipping her face up to mine. "My mom what, Charlie?"

She rolled her lips inward, the edges of her straight white teeth scraping along her bottom lip before it popped free. "Got this."

She swept her hand along her body and I tensed, my initial confusion about my mother settling into a pang of disappointment.

I had every reason to go head-to-head with Charlie. She'd been fucking with me unfettered for over a decade because, no matter what she did, you didn't pay back your best friend's little sister. Especially when you had four years on her and were old enough to know better. Well into adulthood and careers now, I had the freedom to shed the kid gloves. But now that I could, she revealed this hint of insecurity and it stole every bit of thunder in doing so.

I'd never paid too much attention to the dynamic between our parents, but I was watching now—to prove her wrong or me right, I didn't know.

With my hand settled over her lower back, I led her to the far side of the room, to the same table our parents reserved year after year. I pulled out the chair closest to the fireplace, where I knew she preferred to sit. Something about the crackle of the fire or something like that.

The year she turned twenty-one, the last time Chance was with us, she barely touched her food. Instead, she sat there facing the fire, her feet up on her chair, her knees to her chest, a hot toddy in her hands. Firelight danced along her warm brown waves, catching on the natural copper strands threaded throughout. She'd shut out the world and just basked in being, all flushed cheeks from the alcohol, with a smattering of freckles. I'd never seen her so at peace, with the flicker of mischief still lingering distantly in her luminous eyes.

I hadn't seen her like that since. Until now, I hadn't even recognized I'd been trying to catch a glimpse of her like that again. Soft, almost languid, with simmering spunk.

We'd work on that.

Why did I suddenly care? I wasn't sure I wanted to know.

I cupped her elbow and turned her to me before she could sit. She'd lost a bit of her shine back there. The mischief waned in her eyes. The exchange with our moms wormed its way in and whispered lies to her. A part of her bought the bullshit they sold.

But for the next week, she was mine. Mine to care for, to protect, and I needed to get my ass in gear and pay closer attention.

For the time being, what hurt her, hurt me. We were a unit. Tighter than the ones we were born to.

"Charlie." My voice came out thick, almost gritty

with disuse which defied logic since we'd been talking ever since we met up in the parking lot. I tucked my fist under her jaw, brushed my thumb over the tip of her chin, and tipped her face up to mine. "Just so you and I are clear…" I swallowed against the lump in my throat making my words gruff. "There's nothing wrong with this."

Her lips parted on a surprised gasp.

The sound crawled right inside me. That was the only explanation for why I tugged over her bottom lip, pulling it just a touch away from her teeth before letting it snap back.

This wasn't a display for our parents. It wasn't for Mariah and Daniel. This was ours and what it meant, I had no idea.

But damn. Now, I wanted to find out.

I leaned in, my breath fluttering over the shell of her ear, making her shiver against me. "Now sit."

For once, she did as she was told with no comment. I could get used to this. Who knew off-balance Charlie could be so docile. I took my seat next to her and studied the menu despite the constant suspicious glances from the little demon.

Some of us didn't need ghost peppers and scissors.

I smiled.

5
NICK

Our fathers chatted at the other end of the round twelve-top table, bringing their work right into the holiday trip with them as they always did. Profit margins, investments, scaling up businesses, yada yada. Our mothers usually settled into light gossip about mutual friends. Who was getting married, having kids, which ones bought a winter place in Florida —and of course the ones not doing well—hospital stays, new medications, and rehab. With all those topics exhausted, they'd soon try to finesse bankruptcy gossip from our dads.

But so far this year… silence. Mrs. McAllister's gaze bore a hole into us and my mother… well, she'd taken an intense interest in the menu, and from her pinched expression, shit played the starring role in every dish.

Her eyes cut in our direction, a look of pure disapproval landing right on Charlie, prompting fiery anger I never thought I'd feel toward my mom.

"Good evening, ladies and gentlemen. I'm Jeremy. I'll be your server tonight…"

Charlie's leg bounced next to me. With every lift of her heel, her knee brushed mine.

Brush, brush, brush, brush…

Chaotic energy bubbled from her until I was sure she would launch like a rocket straight from her chair at any moment.

When I glanced over, I caught her sneaking a peek at my mother.

I reached over and laid my palm on her thigh, only I overshot, and my fingers curled around the inside of her leg. My breath stuttered in my lungs with the contact. Chance, that fucker… this was all his fault. None of this was in my head. Not a single thought of Charlie in that way and all it took was one ill-advised text conversation I, unfortunately, started to send us down this road to— well, I didn't know where, but the week loomed in front of me like a bad omen as the heat from her thigh warmed my palm.

My fingers flexed ever so slightly.

She gasped, the sharp intake of breath making her breasts thrust out.

Big mistake.

And it was too late to change my mind.

I slapped a smile over every warning bell blaring in my skull and gave her a reassuring squeeze, ignoring the way my blood spiked. A few seconds later, I slid my hand down to her knee where I kept it until I felt the tension radiating from her come to a head, and finally its release with a barely perceptible sigh.

So much for the hand on the lower back leading her

into the room… we just blew right past that part into some weird space where we plunged forward too far, then yanked ourselves back.

There was no way I would share a bed with her. Nope. Was not going to happen. The room better be a double.

After our moms ordered, the waiter turned his attention to Mariah, who ordered salmon and a house salad. Hold the dressing.

She looked like her order, and again, I wondered what I was thinking when I succumbed to a week with her. It was the longest week of my life. Every moment, I learned something new about her, something ugly that made it nearly impossible to tolerate her. She worshipped at the altar of manipulation and tactical maneuvers. Every action designed to attain power. Mariah's efforts to hook me were never about me; they were about connections. I represented another rung on the ladder to status and influence.

Too bad she hadn't taken a closer look.

I came from a successful family, but their success was just that. Theirs. It was clearly a concept she hadn't grasped in the circles she traveled in. Not for the first time, I wondered what my mother was thinking for pushing this match anyway. Mariah's father was one of my father's biggest competitors. They had a rivalry that bordered on unhealthy more often than not. It wasn't like they were going to merge or all of a sudden become fast friends just because their kids married.

For Mariah's part in this, she had likely never looked

beyond my family's success into my actual clientele. I was not my father. I respected him. I learned everything I know from him, but my motivations and vision of success were all my own. As a financial planner for individuals, I focused more on the middle class. I made money, but my bank account would never be as wealthy as my parents, something I was fine with as long as I felt good about my job.

I'd recently taken consulting contracts for larger companies on a case-by-case basis. It wasn't to make my bank account fatter. It wasn't about my own retirement one day. It served as a way to help more people. The minute I took my first contract, I upped my pro bono client percentage from five percent to ten.

Everything about the decision felt right. Two-parent working families trying to plan for their children's college and their eventual retirement. Others wanting to stretch what seemed like a great financial portfolio, unless one of them or their children came down with a chronic illness.

I helped the people in the gray area. The ones who didn't have a fat enough portfolio to interest your average investors. They were the most vulnerable. They had a good start, but no one to teach them how to nurture it.

But they had me now, and I took care of their money like it was my own. And at the end of the day, I knew my job helped real people find stability instead of lining the pockets of the rich.

Mariah definitely wouldn't approve.

I caught a glimpse of Charlie narrowing her eyes at the menu, sporting an evil little grin.

Somehow, I thought she would.

"I'll take the ribeye," Charlie said next to me, pulling me out of my thoughts.

"Charlie, dear…" Her mother began, the sound of her voice making me tense. "Don't you think something a little lighter would be best?"

I eyed the hand Mrs. McAllister laid on Charlie's wrist, her condescending lilt grating on my nerves.

"And the twice-baked potato," Charlie added, completely ignoring her mother—if you didn't notice the way her hand had balled into a fist on the table.

Mariah grinned, her expression cruelly victorious. I'd never lay my hand on a woman, but for a split second, I entertained the idea of watching Charlie whoop her skinny little ass.

"All those carbs. They'll go straight to your—"

Nope. *Nope.* I couldn't do it. "I'll have what she's having, please, and add an extra side of a twice-baked potato." My voice left no argument. Charlie's stiff shoulders relaxed with my words as a breath of tension whispered from between her lips. Her fist opened until her palm lay flat on the table.

Mariah sighed with a roll of her eyes and Mrs. McAllister's mouth snapped shut… a welcome victory.

How often did she deal with this shit? Had this happened before in front of me and I just didn't notice? Christ, my mother never would have treated me like that.

But what about my sister, Holly?

I'd never really paid attention, but now I had to wonder.

The conversation resumed. Charlie's dad asked me about my investment firm and my direction in the company. The ice thawed between our mothers enough to spark a discussion about the expansion of the golf course at their country club and the memorial garden they'd been planning. Even Daniel and Mariah took part in the chatter, but none of them, not a one, asked about Charlie.

What the hell?

And the minute the food arrived, Charlie just stared at it.

She'd eat it. She was too defiant not to, but the shit her mother said would be there in every bite.

Well, I could fix that.

Grabbing my fork, I reached over and scooped up a good-sized bite of the potato from her plate. Whipped and fluffy with sour cream, the crust dotted with apple-wood smoked bacon over cheddar cheese, I made sure I got a bit of everything.

Her gaze locked on that first bite, and her tongue darted out to brush her lips.

Yeah, she wanted it. And she deserved to have it without a heaping of guilt.

Turning toward her, I curled my hand around her neck and waited for her to meet my eyes. "Come here."

Glassy eyes met mine before dropping to my mouth.

My gut bottomed out.

My parents worked hard to instill manners and responsibility in me.

PDA? A huge no-no. But right here, right now, I wanted to take a note from Charlie's playbook and add a little defiant shock value to the evening. Fueled by an underlying current of disdain for her mother's words, I said fuck-all to the lessons in propriety and captured her smart mouth in a determined kiss.

Every goddamned sound faded away to the echo of our breath mingling between us and the drum of my heart pounding behind my ribs.

Her flavor? Bad decisions and mango ChapStick with a hint of my-life-will-never-be-the-same.

At the sound of the squeak from her throat, I squeezed my fingers over the column of her velvety neck, my thumb resting over the spot where her heart-beat raced under her skin.

As a true glutton for punishment, I nipped at that bottom lip before letting her go.

Forehead pressed to hers, I smiled at her dazed expression. "Now, open that smart mouth of yours and eat the potato, Charlie."

Her lips parted, and I settled the fork on her tongue, never taking my gaze off her mouth. My chest squeezed, and my jeans shrunk a couple of sizes, suspiciously only in the zipper area, as her lips closed around the fork. Time slowed, every last second of feeding her searing itself into my brain. With a low, sultry hum, she dragged her mouth back until the tines popped from between her plump lips.

Fuck my life.

I shifted and silently cursed myself.

Before dinner, sharing a room had been an annoyance.

But now… now five nights had danger written all over it.

And despite every warning flashing through my brain like a light machine at a rave, I didn't have even one ounce of self-preservation to stop the gruff words that came next.

"Good girl."

6
Charlie

What the hell was that?

Okay, so I had a lapse in confidence. My mother made comments all the time, and usually I let them roll off, but in the wake of the judgment from Nick's mother, and Daniel and Mariah having a front-row seat, I just—I don't know. My brain farted, okay?

Then her saint of a son stuffed me with potato. My potato, his potato, the communal potato.

And now I never wanted to feed myself again.

My feminism swooned and crumpled in a heap between us. When I tried to pick her up, she flitted off like Peter Pan's elusive shadow.

The backstabbing little bitch.

I pushed through the door to our room, Nick strolling along behind me with his hands casually in his pockets like nothing had happened.

Like he didn't just feed me. *Feed me!*

Like he hadn't just, in spite of the food judgment and in the classiest way possible, made me want that fucking potato again. As though he hadn't all but told me to lie back and relax my pretty little head about it because he lived to serve.

I couldn't be the only one affected here. I refused. I would not be one of the many women falling over tits up for him.

No.

My gaze settled on my garment bag hanging casually in the closet courtesy of the concierge and a slow grin spread over my face, the answer to having the upper hand suddenly clear.

Poor Saint Nick.

He was about to have a rough night.

He pulled the cushions off the couch one at a time, the confusion written on his face morphing into dread. "It's not a bed."

I moved the bag to the hook on the inside of the bathroom door and glanced at him over my shoulder. "The bed is right there."

"There's only one."

"Look at you, you can count."

"I'm not sharing the bed with you, Charlie."

Jesus. I might need him to start calling me Charlotte, no matter how much I loathed the name. Now that I heard the low rumble of my name on his lips as he fed me, I *only* heard my name in that tone.

Nick feeding me was far more intimate than sleeping next to me, but whatever. I shrugged and grasped the zipper. "Fine, take the couch."

"It's scratchy."

I blew out a breath that came out as a half sigh, half

laugh. "So be a grown-up and just sleep on the damn bed, Nick."

"With you?"

"It's a king size. I think we can manage. Why, think you can't resist me?"

What I was about to do was rather cruel considering his current crisis, but I'd ask forgiveness later.

Actually, I would rather go down in flames.

I dragged the zipper in one long pull around all three sides and let it fall open, my gaze on him the whole time.

Mr. Composed, *I'm totally going to rock your russet world* disappeared right before my eyes. Saint Nick, the one who was definitely not so fun at parties, appeared complete with wide eyes and his mouth hanging open.

Over six feet of rock-hard athletic body, forearms for days, and a fucking beard made for riding covering a square jaw so bloody sexy it made clits ache with a single glance stood there, absolutely speechless.

He raised a finger and tilted his head as though he planned to say something, but then his mouth snapped shut.

A muscle ticked in his cheek.

His ass landed on the couch with a thud.

He settled his steepled fingers against his lips while sliding me a sidelong glance.

Some people traveled with twice as many clothes as they needed. Some with an array of makeup cases equipped with colors for any event.

Me… I brought a self-love arsenal that would make

a repressed mama's boy's ass pucker with just one glimpse. "Don't be scared, Saint Nick. They're for me, not you."

His eyebrows shot up in disbelief. "All of them? How many holes you got?"

I laughed. "Some are more accommodating than others and capable of taking on multiples. The female body is rather amazing like that." I rolled my lips over my teeth to stifle my laugh at the strangled sound coming from the man behind me.

"I'm not getting in that bed with you," he said with a hint of censure in his tone.

"Suit yourself."

I grabbed my pajamas and ducked into the bathroom. The fan muffled my giggle while I dragged my jeans down my thighs. I'd bet I'd find him in the same spot when I finished.

Good. I would not be off-balance by myself. Especially since this sharing-a-room thing totally killed my weekend plans to diddle my skittle on every luxury surface imaginable.

I dragged a brush through my hair and threw it up in a messy knot on my head before I washed my face, brushed my teeth, and tossed out my contacts.

A few minutes later and feeling more like me than I had since I arrived, I found Nick leaning back on the couch, a bottle of vodka tipped to his lips. His gaze was locked on the garment bag as it rocked back and forth from the force of me whipping the door open.

The first bottle lay empty on the coffee table, and he clutched a third in his other hand.

"Poor Saint Nick. I drove you to drink."

"If this were any other year, I'd be at the bar right now."

"So, go. No one's stopping you."

"This relationship," he said, making an air quote gesture with his fingers, "is stopping me. You really want our moms to see me drinking alone?"

I shrugged and peeled back the covers of the bed. "There could be a lot of reasons for you to be there alone. Watching a game. I have a headache. I got my period. Maybe you stuffed me with so much potato there's no room right now for your eggplant." With potato fantasies still playing in my brain, I shot him a smirk, my gaze landing on his zipper. "Or maybe you're more of a baby carrot kind of guy."

"Judging by the size of the holes you cut out of my pants, shorts, and boxers, you had eggplant fantasies." His lips curled down in the corners with a sarcastic edge I wasn't used to seeing on him but actually kind of liked on account of the expression proved he was human like the rest of us. "Either way, there's only one way you'd ever find out, and that's if I lose my mind and decide to smack your smart mouth with it."

The picture he painted was so out of left field with his personality, I choked on a ball of laughter. Tears sprang to my eyes. I slapped my palms against the bed and doubled over with a wheeze.

"The day you smack anyone with your dick is the

day I'll let a dude tell me what to do." When I finally managed to look up at him and breathe again, a look I'd never seen crossed his face, and the last of the laughter died on my lips. Trapped by his heavy gaze, I swallowed the lump in my throat.

Neither of us looked away, but he finally blinked and the tension snapped.

Goddamn potato hallucinations. That's all this was. It had to be.

"Good to know, Charlie," he said quietly.

The words hung in the air like a fucking promise, but a promise of what?

"Why don't you ever go to the bar with us?" he asked as he flopped his head back on the couch and stared up at the ceiling.

"Because Chance can't handle the fact that I fuck about as often as he does." Met with silence, I settled under the covers and glanced over to find him staring at me.

Hard.

"What?"

"Do you?" he asked. The muscles in his cheek jumped.

Huh.

"Do I?"

"Fuck as often as he does?"

It was like he was seeing me for the first time. No bullshit antics. No defense mechanisms. He was looking at me like a man looked at a woman.

His gaze crawled over me, and I shrugged like it

wasn't a big deal, despite the way my heart raced in response.

"What's my motivation to lie? What translates to big dick energy for you guys is branded promiscuity for me, so the truth doesn't exactly make me look good."

His Adam's apple bobbed when he swallowed, and he nodded, his eyes flicking back to the bag. "The big one. I don't—" He shook his head and gulped down more vodka. "That one confuses me."

"Ahh, this sucker." I hopped up and slid it out of the long mesh accessory pocket and held it up with both hands. "This is the Wanachi Mega Massager." I gave it a swing and slapped the head into my palm, the snap echoing in the room. "She's a girthy one, right? Seventeen inches long. The head is four and a half inches tall on its own."

This—humor—felt like safe ground.

He ran his fingers through his hair. "You're a massage therapist."

"Yeeeeeessss."

"But a regular one, right? You don't—you're not—"

He gestured to his lap, and I couldn't help but laugh. "Not what? Into happy endings?"

"Yeah." He drained the rest of the little bottle in his hand.

"On my own? Sure. But I'm not a sex worker." I shrugged. "No judgment. Just not my thing."

"So this weekend you planned to—" He waved his arm but didn't say the words.

The vodka had definitely started taking hold, and

apparently, I was just going to keep filling in the blanks. "Masturbate?

He blinked, opened his mouth, snapped it shut, then blinked again.

I grinned. "Yes."

"Jesus."

"Everyone does it."

"I know but—"

I dropped the massager on the mattress and plopped down next to it. "Even you, Nick. I bet you do it more than the rest of us."

"Charlie," he growled with a glare aimed my way.

I crept my fingertips over the curve of the wand and wiggled my eyebrows. "You into long showers, Nick?"

"Shut it, Charlie." He slammed the empty bottle on the table and leaned forward, dropping his elbows on his knees. "God, your brother is a real asshole for not being here."

"Wanna fuck with him?"

He dragged his fingers through his hair and his gaze snapped up to mine. "What do you mean?"

"How do you think he'd feel about us rooming together?"

"He'd hate it." He shook his head and his lips twitched. "God, would he hate the hell out of it."

"Exactly. Come here." I patted the bed and waited for him to make his way over. He caught himself on the corner and steadied himself before shuffling between the wall and mattress.

"God, that shit is going straight to your head, isn't it?"

"Yes, thank fuck." Weaving on his feet, his gaze landed on my boobs. "You're not wearing a bra."

"They're just boobs, Nick. Your mom has them."

His eyes squeezed shut. A flush spread over his cheeks, the liquor warming him from the inside out.

Off-balance Nick was actually kind of fun to watch.

"Nope. No talking about anything on my mother or father. Nada."

"God, you must be fun in the bedroom. Yeesh." I unlocked my phone. "Take your shirt off."

He didn't even argue, which told me just how hard the liquor was hitting him. Good, the sphincter would stop being so stubborn and just sleep in the bed.

His black Henley hit the floor.

My mouth ran dry.

Dark hair curled over his hard chest, narrowing to a trail running along the valley of his abdomen and disappearing behind his zipper to the thick bulge there.

Ummm…

He flicked open the button of his jeans, his eyes following my gaze as I followed the hair even farther down.

He smirked. "I'm not hard."

He said it like he was proud of the fact. Proud of that super self-control. And all I could think was if he was that big and not hard, how big was he when—not the point.

I shook my head. *Snap out of it, hussy.* "Good to know, Romeo. Come on… selfie time."

"And…" he trailed off, pointing a finger at me. "You might be surprised by how I am in the bedroom. Shocked even." He dropped onto the bed and scooted in next to me.

"Sure, I would." I snorted and slung my arm over his shoulders and angled the lens just right. With the alcohol swirling in his gut, he might have thought he talked a good game, but I was not biting. "Now smile."

Chance was going to lose his shit, and I couldn't be happier. I was perfectly sober, but Nick was sporting a super cozy buzz and he'd leaned into me in a way I knew Chance had never seen before. In the background, the toy collection hung on the door promising one hell of a night.

Ah, solid ground. Charlie, the troublemaker, perfectly sober, plying Saint Nick with alcohol and seducing him into a night of debauchery.

I tossed a tongue emoji on it and typed ROOMIES! in all caps before sending it off.

Then I silenced my cell. *Have a good night, bro.*

"God, I'm tired," he muttered next to me.

"You're lit."

He gave me a thumbs-up and dropped his arm just to have his fingers land on the massager. His eyebrows drew together, and he yanked his hand back.

Not lit enough, apparently. I grabbed it and held it up between us. "Don't be scared… if you're so worried about your virtue, this is your best friend."

"That looks like a goddamned virtue collector for a giant."

"Ha! Good one. The fear in your eyes means you won't cross it. Your virtue is safe. You were so worried about my vagina having teeth, but see, no teeth marks."

He stretched and his jeans slid lower. "We're sleeping with it?"

I glanced up at his face. His face was safe. Except his head lolled in my direction. His eyes slid closed partway, and a sloppy grin played over his mouth.

The mouth that had kissed the fucking breath clean out of me at dinner in front of everyone. A kiss that despite logic, I wanted to do all over again. "Yup. Right between us. He enjoys being the little spoon."

He let out a deep, grating laugh that had my nipples pebbling painfully hard under my tank top. Saint Nick transformed into Stunningly Sexy Nick in that moment and knocked the air from my lungs.

I blamed the potatoes for this.

7
Charlie

All those who got a good night's sleep, raise your hand. Oh look, not a single hand in the air. That tracks.

I dragged my weary ass to the coffee bar and grabbed a steaming cup of confidence. No way I was joining the table without something to keep me on my toes. A tall cup of coffee with a shot of espresso would ensure I conjured up the perfect comeback at just the right time should the need arise.

It always did, without fail.

The minute I walked into the room, Nick's mom's eyes landed on me and hadn't stopped tracking me since. Our families did everything together growing up. Summers spent at the lake with huge barbecues, boating, and bonfires. Winters on the slopes not only here but on family trips to Utah and Colorado.

I'd never once felt like a pariah with the McAdams family. My family, sure, that's what happened when you were one of three kids who all went off and became who they were in their hearts and not who their mother wanted them to be. My choices never seemed to bother

Nick's mother, but then, she'd never had to worry about me being anything other than her best friend's daughter.

My mom had likely spent the better part of their night gushing over my conquest with my dad. I could only imagine the choice things Nick's mom said to him.

Maybe I'd test all the waters this morning. I grabbed a monster Danish. Lots of calories. Fat for days. Turning to the table, I spotted Daniel taking a seat, his eyes finding me almost immediately.

What the fuck was he up to anyway?

To say we hadn't ended well would be a colossal understatement. He cheated, I caught him, and instead of raving like a lunatic or exacting public revenge like so many women would, I went straight for very personal revenge.

It made me wonder if he was really here hoping to find a way back in with me or if my mother summoning him had everything to do with payback.

Cool and calculated, a quality I liked about him at first, until I didn't, he tracked my every move as I weaved through the tables toward them.

No blinking. Not even a hint of a smile.

Payback for sure.

Something told me to avoid being alone with him… because he might just push my ass off a lift or something.

Okay, so I kind of regretted coming down without Nick now. Not so he could protect me, but buddy system and all that. Witnesses were a good thing.

When I arrived at the table, my dad was right there to smile and kiss my cheek and Nick's dad followed suit.

"You look ready to conquer a few black diamonds today," my father said, tucking me in under his arm.

"You know it." I leaned into him, laying my head against his chest for the briefest of moments before glancing up. "How about you? You want to take on The Dagger with me?"

He was already shaking his head before I finished the question.

"I'm going to leave that trail to you, young lady." He gave my shoulders a squeeze. "Skis or snowboard today?"

I leaned into the affection—needing it, taking from it what I no longer got from my mother. "The board. Every day."

Giving me one last squeeze, he let me go. "You be careful."

"Always." This was why I preferred hanging out with the guys. No passive-aggressive comments. Just straight shooters.

Now to see how Nick had done at shutting down my mother.

She'd always been careful about her figure. And while she'd made a few comments over the years, she'd never been quite so blatant and never in front of others. Or at least in front of nonfamily. Daniel and Mariah having a front-row seat only added insult to injury, leaving me choking on bitterness.

My mom acted as though my eating red meat and a potato would send Nick running for the hills.

If it had that effect on him, I didn't want him anyway. Plus, Nick would never do that to me. If anything, Nick was solid. A rock of dedication. He'd never betray—

God, I'm talking like he's really my boyfriend and this isn't just some convenient way to avoid two assholes who actually would be rather good for each other.

If they'd stop looking at us and start looking at each other, we could all take a damn breath already.

I pulled out the chair next to my mom and slapped the Danish down between us with a snap of attitude.

She did a double take, her lips pinching together before she finally smiled. "Where's Nick?"

Mrs. McAdams glanced over, her attention one hundred percent on my answer despite Mariah still chatting beside her.

"I tired him out last night," I said with a wink, unable to resist goading Nick's mom. "He's sleeping in."

"Oh, I—*Oh*!" My mom's hand flew to her chest and her cheeks turned pink.

Ewww.

The sheer joy on my mother's face at the idea that I rode Nick, stayed on for more than eight seconds and stuck the landing, which had bile climbing up the back of my throat.

"Yes, best to let him sleep then." The sheer delight on her face stood in stark contrast to whatever the hell was going on with Mrs. McAdams's expression.

I tore off a piece of pastry and popped it into my mouth, holding Mrs. McAdams's gaze the entire time.

My mother positively bubbly about my not-so-sexy sex life with Nick? Now that was one I didn't have on my bingo card.

She offered not one peep about the food since clearly, I had spent the night servicing my man, and I intended to ride that high as far as it would take me. If I didn't plan to take on the hardest trail on the mountain, The Dagger, I'd let it walk me right back to the coffee bar for a second Danish.

She didn't need to know I'd spent my night tossing and turning, studying him in the dark every time my eyes popped open, which seemed to be about every hour.

Still under the influence of the potato, no doubt.

I traced over his every feature. The dark, wavy hair smoothed back from his forehead and the disgustingly long lashes a woman would kill for. Stretched out on his back, he fell asleep where he lay, his hand up over his head, the other drawing my gaze to where his palm rested against the deep V carved along his abs, his long fingers curled along his jeans brushing the bulge behind his zipper.

Every time he stretched, I held my breath, waiting to see if the waistband slid lower.

By the time early morning filtered through the gauzy curtains, I had a seething lady boner and a raging clit shaking her angry fist.

God, but he was beautiful and so very different from... well, anyone.

Any other time, I would have just grabbed a toy or two, disappeared into the bathroom, and taken care of business, but I couldn't bring myself to give up the view. I probably should have just touched myself right there beside him. He slept like the dead.

But by the time I got out of bed, he'd finally shifted, and the position was photographic gold. I ducked out while he was in the shower, but not before sending Chance another message while ignoring his litany of threats in dozens of others.

I pushed his buttons on the other side of the world and pushed a few more here. Hey, I took my normalcy where I could get it.

A firm hand landed on my shoulder and squeezed.

"Good morning." Nick aimed the words at the table before bending down and stopping right next to my cheek. His hand drifted to my neck, his fingers tangling in the ends of my ponytail, giving it a firm tug. This was the second time he'd pulled my hair, and Jesus fuck, this was so going to be my new fantasy. He turned me toward him just enough to settle his lips along the shell of my ear.

"You're in so much trouble, spawn. When I get you alone, it's payback time."

My nipples tightened to painful points.

Saint Nick must have checked his messages from Chance.

The low rasp of his voice vibrated over me. Warm,

minty breath brushed along my skin, sending a powerful burn singing through my blood. The two conspired against me, tapping into the unfulfilled, furious lust from my long horny night stuck between my beloved toy arsenal and Nick's hard, languid body.

He drew my face to his and soundly claimed my mouth in a slow, deep kiss. His tongue caressed mine with unhurried long strokes while his fingertips kneaded my flesh. The combination left me a puddle of humming, aroused mush slumping in my seat.

A little over twelve hours ago, I told Nick he couldn't handle me.

Now I had to wonder if I could handle him.

It took one potato and two bone-melting kisses before I realized the game we were playing. Every time I thought I had the upper hand, he'd strike.

So far, the score was his three to my zero.

What the fuck had I started?

8
NICK

The second kiss told me I was in deep shit.

What was supposed to be a private word of warning for the picture she snapped of me in the early morning hours *and* a sign of affection for the table became possession.

The minute I tasted her again, it sparked a craving.

The mini bar was powerless to erase her taste. I spent a disgusting amount of time in the shower, fucking my fist, biting my forearm to keep her name from spilling from my lips.

Satisfyingly dissatisfied, yeah, I know, it made no sense, but here we were. And when I was done, I stepped out of the bathroom to find her gone.

In the silence of our room, her brown sugar and vanilla voodoo body wash scent still lingering, want flooded me. In that singular moment, the only thing I could think about was when I could taste her again.

Ignoring everyone at the table including my own parents—definitely unlike me—I reached for her. And if anyone was unclear about where I stood with Charlie McAllister, they weren't now.

My fake girlfriend got less and less fake with every laugh, every touch, and every shared breath.

Fuck me.

Now, snapping my boot into my binding, with a breakfast I don't remember tasting swirling in my gut, her kiss lingered despite every bold flavor I'd pummeled my tongue with since.

The condition better not be permanent.

With my second boot snapped in, I pushed off, ski skating my way over to the lift where Charlie waited in line.

"You took off without me."

She peeled the straps out of her helmet and settled it on her head. "You were in the shower for a really long time, Nick. With all my toys. Coincidence?"

I watched her fumble with the clasp under her chin because naturally, she tried to do it the hard way… with her gloves still on. "I don't need toys."

She dropped her arms with a frustrated huff. "Went old school and used your hand. That sounds like you. Classic."

"What's that supposed to mean?"

"Just an observation. You're simple. Polite. Keepin' it vanilla with the self-love. It's all… well, consistent." She gave my shoulder a condescending pat. "Very you."

I tugged her straps and dragged her toward me until her board stopped between my skis, and I loomed over her. My proximity forced her to crane her neck to meet my eyes.

Good.

What was it about the short and curvy ones? They had mouths on them. All of them. And if I didn't know better, I'd swear it was some worldwide underground cult, and Charlie was their fearless leader.

"Keep it up and you're going to find out just how impolite I can be." Tension settled in the ridge of my shoulders. How easy it would be to just lower my mouth a few more inches and take another taste.

Hovering over her, I took in her heavy eyelids and the loaded glance flicked to my mouth.

"No need for the show," she whispered. "There's no one around to see it."

I breathed her in. "Maybe it's not for them, maybe—"

"Well, aren't you two cozy," Daniel said, skidding to a stop right next to us.

I dropped my hands, and her head swung in his direction. "Fuck off, Daniel."

The laugh was out before I could stop it, earning a hard glance from Charlie's ex.

"So much energy," he sneered. "Is Nick not burning that off with you between the sheets? Too bad. She can be a real wildcat—"

Something in me, something I didn't recognize, snapped and the sound that came out of me was unlike anything I'd ever unleashed. My arm shot out, and I curled my fist in his jacket, dragging him right up to my side. I took particular pleasure in watching the asshole struggle to stay upright on his skis. "Finish what you're about to say and you leave in an ambulance. Got it?"

Charlie gasped.

Daniel puffed out his chest. As much as he could with me keeping him immobile and off-kilter. "Bring it."

"Nope. You guys are not doing this shit."

"She's right," Daniel said. "How about we make this dignified? The Dagger. First one to the bottom wins."

"We haven't even done a practice run yet," Charlie said.

"You need one, Nick?" he asked with that smug smirk on his mouth. "I don't, but hey, I can wait if you want to get a run or two in if you think you need the practice."

This son of a bitch. He'd had his eyes on me, and definitely on us, but had he spent any time focusing on Charlie in all that time?

No.

Because he didn't want her. She was reduced to a toy he'd cast aside that he suddenly wanted to play with the minute someone else showed interest. He needed to control her. Nothing more, nothing less.

To him, she was merely a possession.

Couldn't he see she was the last woman on the planet to let a man possess her? Or did he just not care?

Maybe that was the challenge.

It stopped here.

I nodded and let go of his jacket with a hard shove back, sending his arms flailing to gain his balance. "Let's go."

The chilly ride to the top of the mountain took a total of eight minutes. Eight minutes of Daniel whistling on one side of the quad like he already had this in the bag and Charlie shooting daggers at both of us while muttering the word "idiots" as often as possible in between.

"This is stupid and juvenile," she bit out.

I leaned in, having no doubt the fucker would try to listen. "He won't stop until someone puts him in his place."

"I've got news for you, Nick. I know him a lot better than you do and even then, he will not stop."

The words only served to remind me that she actually spent time in a relationship with this prick. I wasn't easy to piss off, but the image of them skidded uninvited into my head, his hands all over her—her kissing him back, rising over him. *Fuck.* The ache in my balled fists pulled me out of the scene, but not before some fucked-up urge to mark her as mine took root in my head.

She had the worst taste in guys. Daniel was just one of a handful, and none of them were good enough for her. On that Chance and I agreed. Between the two of us, it had been a full-time job chasing off the fuckers sniffing around her.

My thoughts wandered to my sister, Holly—how I had yet to scare off any guys. There hadn't been any. Right?

She was a hell of a lot younger than me and not part of my parents' plan so maybe I was too wrapped up in graduate school to notice the guys orbiting around her when she started high school.

That had to be it. Because it would be weird if I chased dudes away from my best friend's little sister but didn't for my own.

9

NICK

Only a handful of skiers joined us on the single most dangerous trail on the mountain. Hairpin turns leading into dangerous narrow sections wide enough for just one left little room for passing. Whoever took the early lead would hold the edge for most of the ride.

Steep inclines, and craggy rock outcroppings jutting out over those sections, only upped the stakes. If you made it through all of that, moguls lay in wait, ready to attack your body until your teeth rattled.

Charlie shuffled over and grabbed the front of my jacket, pulling me in close.

"Baby, if you want one more kiss, all you have to do is say so," I said, unable to resist the opportunity to get under her skin.

"God, you're a boob. Listen——" She hooked her gloved hand through the goggles on my helmet and yanked my head down to hers. "He cheats. He loves the hairpins, but he sucks at moguls."

I glanced at where Daniel stood watching us. "Got

it. Does this mean you're okay with me kicking his ass now?"

She glanced over her shoulder, her lips flattened with irritation. "Kick his ass, but you'll still only be in second place because I'm taking you both out." She nipped at my upper lip and darted her tongue out to swipe my bottom lip before she released my goggles, letting them snap against my helmet.

Daniel wasn't the only cheater. The kisses were for show, but fuck, my dick did not get the memo. I'd been hard at least four times now with no damn relief. I'd be walking funny by tomorrow if I didn't give my partner in crime a little one-on-one. "That's my girl."

For now.

I shot a wink at the asshole ex, my hand sliding off Charlie's ass—a move I hadn't noticed I made, and I grinned. He didn't stand a chance.

On the count of three, we took off. Actually, the asshole jumped the start because he was an absolute shitbag.

What Charlie ever saw in that guy, I'd never know. He was good-looking enough, I supposed. A full head of hair and in shape, but his character reeked of deep rot.

Tucking low, I launched down the first hill, taking every bit of speed the packed snow would give me. In a matter of seconds, we'd veer left into unpredictable territory riddled with danger.

The wide ninety-degree turn narrowed from thirty feet wide to ten at most. The angle of the turn and outer lip created a slingshot effect, scooping us right along with it and pitching us diagonally down a three-foot-wide ledge along a rock face overlooking the beginner and intermediate trails unfolding down the mountain.

From the vantage point below, this part of The Dagger looked like a Hot Wheels track attached to a wall, with us shooting across toward Devil's corner where we'd have to jump to make the one-hundred-and-fifty-degree sharp right, shooting back the other way before pitching us into the wooded wasteland, a section littered with trees and rock and completely ungroomed.

I dug in my edge, shaving off a bit of speed, but ready to take the corner and stay tight on Daniel's skis.

Still thirty feet short of the turn, I spotted Charlie's teal jacket out of the corner of my eye before she dropped over the edge.

The air lodged in my lungs. My ski bobbled, but with another glance, I saw her land on the trail below and shoot straight out of sight.

Fuck, but my heart.

She learned the trick from Chance, and she'd gotten good at it on the board. I knew she'd jump the corner, but I never expected her to push it and take on a fifteen-foot drop this soon just to get ahead.

Daniel and I both cut hard right, catching our edges deep, before twisting our shoulders and pushing off at the knees.

The minute we made it through the treacherous turns, I gained on him through the trees. He followed the path already cut by two or three skiers before us, but I shot left where the trees were thicker and stayed low to avoid the branches.

We were head-to-head on the moguls with Charlie's words in my head.

My lungs ached. I kept my knees loose as the force from every bump threatened to shoot straight through my legs into my skull the minute I tensed up.

At the end, I glanced back to find Daniel still fighting the last third of the section. I tucked and crouched low, racing down the trail where it widened out, darting in and out of other skiers. Spotting Charlie, I headed right at her and slid to a hard stop.

Lungs heaving, we both hunched over, sucking in precious gulps of air as Daniel came skidding in last.

He yanked his goggles from his eyes and glared over at us. "Best two out of three."

"Nope, I won. You guys want to do some dick measuring, you're doing it without me," Charlie said as she arched her back and stretched her neck from side to side.

"Give it up, man. You lost."

"Not yet I didn't," he said, baring his teeth. "Two out of three. Now!" He reached out, catching Charlie by surprise when he grabbed her wrist and yanked her toward the lift.

"Hey—" she yelled.

"Get. Your. Hand. Off. Her." Hot piercing anger pounded in my chest. I swung out and knocked his arm away when he didn't let go of her fast enough.

In seconds I was out of my bindings and in his face, forcing his eyes up because I had at least four inches on him. "Fuck with her and find out, Sloan."

His chest swelled with a furious drag of air into his lungs before he bumped into mine. For a minute, he seemed as though he might push me.

Do it.

Fucking do it.

I would love nothing more than to pummel this smarmy bastard's smug face for grabbing her. For ever laying one fucking hand on her.

Was this how he acted when they were a couple? Did he lay a hand on her then too? I couldn't picture her letting anyone get away with abusing her, but then, I never expected to see her hesitate to eat because of some pithy comment from her mother either.

He blinked, his shoulders drooped just slightly, and I knew he'd cave.

I should have let him walk away when he did.

He brought his palms up and took a step back.

"Best two out of three. Now." A muscle ticked in my cheek. I gnashed my teeth so hard my jaw ached to stop the litany of words begging to come out.

With a satisfied nod, he headed for the quad. I knew I'd given him what he wanted, but I was about to obliterate him on The Dagger two more times if it killed me.

"Is that the first time?" The question flew out the minute I was sure Daniel was out of earshot. I snapped my pole against my boot to knock the packed snow off so I could click back into my bindings.

She gripped my jacket. "Nick—"

My gaze flashed to hers. I didn't know what she saw there, but she let me go and swallowed hard.

"Is that the first time he put his hands on you like that?"

"He's still breathing, right?"

"Unfortunately." I bit out the words, seething anger bubbling inside me with nowhere to go. "Yes or no, Charlie? I need to hear it."

"Yes. It's the first time. And last. If it makes you feel any better… he got his before we broke up."

I jammed my heel in the binding until I heard the telltale click. "Good. How?"

"I superglued his dick to his thigh while he slept."

The rage in my chest loosened its grip, and I laughed. "Of course you did. Wow."

"Hey, he cheated." She shrugged with no emotion behind the words. Simple. Direct. One hundred percent Charlie. "This is getting—I don't know. I'm sorry. None of this was supposed to be this complicated."

"No complication. He needs his ass beat. You already did it, but he's a slow learner. I'll finish the job." I grabbed her collar, hauled her up under my mouth, and dropped another kiss on her lips because apparently, I'm racking them up now. "Go have fun."

"You're going to be sore as fuck." She cupped my cheek, and I turned my head and nipped at her thumb.

"That's what hot tubs are for. I'll meet up with you later. We'll talk about that reckless move you pulled up there."

She laughed and shoved me toward the lift. "Can't wait."

10
Charlie

With everyone otherwise occupied, I was able to spend the next couple of hours snowboarding my way, sans all the testosterone, alternating black diamond trails with scenic intermediate blue diamond ones. Switching back and forth would keep my limbs nice and loose.

As for Nick, his would be Jell-O before he even reached the bottom of his third run down The Dagger. He'd win, but it was going to cost him. He was going to cry when he found out the hot tubs were now closed for the day for unexpected maintenance. I almost felt bad for him… since he was doing this for me, but then, like he said, I took care of Daniel myself. Anything beyond was just a dick measuring contest between Nick and Daniel.

Boys.

For me, it was over, just like our mistake of a relationship.

I had to admit though, seeing Nick like this was… a lot. Okay, hot. Not that I would ever admit that out loud, but yes, the hard look on his face, the intense angry stare, it did something for me. Saint Nick with his feathers ruffled, not by me, but by some primitive form of honor and male competition, could slay vajays better than the carefully cultivated collection of toys I'd brought with me.

Whew.

This whole new side of him—maybe it came out because he thought he needed to protect my honor since Chance wasn't here to do it. I didn't know. I probably shouldn't look at it too closely because the lines between us had already blurred more than the vision of a twenty-one-year-old birthday boy sporting his first beer goggles.

I needed him out of my mind, and I needed a damn minute to get my bearings because all the reasons he irritated the shit out of me slipped away more and more by the minute.

So, with a bit of time to myself, I grabbed a bag and headed for the wish tree.

I loved and hated this part.

I loved that I could make a difference for so many and despised my inability to make a difference for all of them. I did my best to choose a combo between boys, girls, and gifts that could really be for the whole family, specifically game systems.

Guesstimating the prices as I went, I tried not to think about the paper angels that would remain here through the holiday, only to be tossed in the trash when the tree came down after New Year's. I reminded myself I was lucky to be able to do this much. My parents covered the cost for the family since it was their tradition, so I had money to play with. Especially since we were all adults now and decided to forgo buying presents for each other.

Instead, we focused on relaxation and laid-back traditions… or I did. My parents worried more about socializing. I soaked up the nonstop skiing, naps in between runs, endless hot chocolate, and real meals I didn't have to make myself. Then there were the hot tubs in the atrium which was basically hot tubbing it in our very own snow globe. Lazy, unstructured days all leading up to the Silent Night Festival on Christmas Eve that ironically was not so silent. It was a big warm room with dim lighting letting the Christmas lights really shine, endless holiday-themed cocktails, fun music, and dancing.

The number on my calculator app finally rolled over five thousand and I sighed. With a nearly full bag, I turned away from the tree, a pinch in my heart leaving an ache I knew I wouldn't shake.

When I finally made it to my room, the minute I got through the door, I flopped onto my bed.

Fifteen minutes. I just needed fifteen minutes. Then I'd make a list and form a game plan so I could get the shopping done in one shot tomorrow morning.

The sound of the sink running had the eye not shoved into my pillow popping open. I pushed up on my elbows and listened. Yup, my sink.

Housekeeping.

There was seriously nothing more uncomfortable

than being in the room while the staff did their thing. I couldn't imagine they liked it either.

With my power nap dreams dashed, I hopped up. "I'm sorry, I didn't realize you were in here, I'll get out of——" I peeked around the corner and the words died on my lips.

Nick stood there, wrapped in nothing but a white towel low on his hips, one hand propped against the sink, while he rinsed his razor with the other. The chest hair I tried but failed to ignore last night, well, it was magnificent when damp. Moisture clung to his shoulders and arms. One single drop broke free and streaked down his biceps right long the predominant ridge made by the flex of the arm bracing his weight.

The green-eyed monster reared up and just like that, I was officially jealous of a water droplet. Before I knew what I was doing, my gaze landed right on his deliciously round ass.

"You were saying?" he asked, giving me a smirk before heading for his neck with the razor.

"Don't shave it!" I slapped both hands over my mouth like I could stuff the words back in. Jesus, why had I blurted that out? What the hell did I care if he shaved? It's his fucking facial hair and had absolutely nothing—*nothing*—to do with me.

His hand froze, and his eyes slid in my direction. That eyebrow of his quirked. "Why not?"

I grasped for something, anything to explain why suddenly that beard was of any importance to me at all.

"Ummm, it's… it's supposed to be really cold over the next few days; it'll keep you warm on the slopes."

Shut up. Shut up. Shut up.

Good God… why didn't you just tell the man you want to ride his face because judging by the laughter dancing in those rich brown eyes, he knew this definitely had nothing to do with his keeping warm.

He set the razor down and turned off the water, his movements calm and purposeful. Stepping into the doorway, he settled a hand over the molding above the door and crooked a finger at me with the other.

I'd swear the bastard got that from TikTok if I didn't know for a fact he loathed all things social media.

My mouth went dry, but my down below flooded in a way that could rival *THE* flood. You know, the one… animals two by two and all that. But there was no ark to save me. Stumbling off the bed, I stepped right up to him and pretended to be unaffected by his, well—his everything.

Wait. He crooked his finger, and I scrambled to get to him. Welp, that would definitely go straight to his head. I needed to get a handle on the power shift and fast. I had a history of knocking Nick off his toes, not the other way around.

"Worried about me staying warm, huh?" he said quietly as he peered down at me. I heard the laughter he held back, and if it didn't mean touching naked skin, I might have just punched him in the gut.

"Wouldn't want you to catch a chill and use it as an excuse to hog all the blankets." Could my comebacks be any more lame right now? If a hole wanted to open right here, right now, and swallow me, I was down. Send me right to hell. I hated the heat, but I'd deal, just save me from myself… *please*!

I had never, *never* been struck stupid around this man. Because why the hell would I ever let him see me like that, where he could lord it over me? What the hell was wrong with me? It was just a towel. Just a few muscles. Chest hair. A happy trail. A deep V heading straight toward his… never mind. And how the hell was his towel staying on his hips? Because the off-kilter knot looked like it could fall apart at any second.

Was there some class these guys took to do that?

I struggled to keep a towel knotted around my baditties.

Yes, baditties.

If it didn't involve him touching me and my certain humiliation making eye contact off limits for at least six months, I might consider having him teach me.

While I was busy having an internal crisis, he took my hand and gave me a tug. "Come on."

My tongue stuck to the roof of my mouth, and I clamped my lips shut in an effort to shut the fuck up since my track history in the past two minutes proved I had nothing clever to say.

He spun me until my back was to the sink and before I realized what he intended to do, his hands locked on my rib cage, and he lifted me onto the counter.

Effortlessly. A fact that totally hit me in the vajayjay.

I was still fighting to take a deep breath because my brain started drooling at the proximity of his thumbs to my breasts when those long fingers closed over the handle of the razor. "You do it."

"You've got to be kidding."

Dropping it in my hand, he nudged my knees farther apart with his left hand and hip.

I couldn't help but look down to see if the knot at his waist slipped any more with the motion.

"Nope. You decide how much stays and how much goes."

Cool to the touch, the textured handle laid heavy in my palm. This wasn't your ordinary disposable razor. It was the kind handed down to you by your father and sure enough, a monogramed M had been carved into the end. "You really want to trust me with a razor to your throat."

He smiled, his hands going to the sink edge on either side of my hips where he leaned until he reached eye level with me. "You won't hurt me… you'd never hear the end of it from our parents."

"Ain't that the truth," I muttered.

"And you like me," he added.

"Well, I don't hate you, but like might be pushing it." This had bad idea stamped all over it. "So, showering midday huh? Tell me you didn't succumb to the succubus and now you're showering her skinny ass off you." My throat grew thick, aching at the thought. I absolutely would not analyze what that meant.

His eyes flashed.

Catching my wrist as I brought the razor up, he halted my movement. "*Tell me* you didn't just ask me that, Charlie."

I wasn't ready for the bite of anger in his voice. "Well, I don't know. You're showering at noon, Nick."

"Because my *girlfriend* took off to breakfast without me this morning, leaving me scrambling to catch up, then I had to whoop her ex's ass for disrespecting her."

It's just a show. Down girl.

It was all just an act. I had better remind myself of the fact every chance I had.

"So you beat him?"

His lips twitched, but he managed to keep the cocky grin most guys would have at bay. "Yeah, I beat him."

I know I loathed the testosterone battle, and boys were basically dumb when they went head-to-head like this, but I still had to chew on my lip to keep from grinning like an idiot.

"Don't do that," he said, brushing his thumb over the spot. "You'll bruise that pretty mouth."

The air grew thick, our eyes locked, and the space between us seemed to have a heartbeat of its own.

I cleared my throat and grasped for solid ground. "Pretty mouth, huh? You sure you wore your helmet the whole time or is this some undiagnosed head injury talking?"

"The only part of me uninjured *is* my head. Since the hot tubs are now closed, I took an hour-long shower so hopefully I'll be able to walk later."

"You're young. You'll be fine," I lied.

"You and I both know that's not true. Three double black diamonds in a row—with moguls—at maximum speed is not the way to start the ski season."

I shrugged. "I can give you a massage."

He scoffed. "Sure, and be at your mercy? Sounds like a good opportunity for you to mess with me."

My smirk was immediate. "I don't need to give you a massage to do that, Nick. I have so many tools at my disposal if I want to fuck with you." My gaze slid to my collection of sex toys, and he winced.

"Fine, I'll consider it, but I'm telling you, *if* I let you and anything from that bag finds any of my holes, you're a dead woman."

"Those toys you're side-eyeing can be just as fun for you as they are for me. But yes, Saint Nick, your virtue is safe with me." I nudged his chin, silently telling him to tilt his head back while I tried not to picture sliding one of my butt plugs in his ass. I bit back the groan and concentrated on where his beard ended and new growth crept in. Laying the razor at the edge of the line, I dragged it carefully through the shaving cream there, in the same direction the hair grew… the way I'd seen my dad and Chance do.

My breath caught. Something about the way the hair resisted the blade sent a delicious shiver down my spine. A little breathless and a lot overheated, I couldn't wait to do it again.

Nick turned the water back on, and I rinsed the blade before going in for another swipe.

The low, almost imperceptible pop of the hairs

slicing away made a deep scraping sound only the two of us could hear.

Scccrrrraaaaaaape.

And just like that, the edge of his Adam's apple came into view.

I fidgeted on the counter against the sensation between my legs.

Scccrrrraaaaaaape.

Now the center as it bobbed with his swallow.

He crept his hand oh-so-slowly up my thigh and squeezed, stilling my bouncing knee.

Scccrrrraaaaaaape.

The toy fantasy was hot, but this… this was—intimate. With the last swipe, the whole middle of his throat lay exposed, the skin so smooth I wanted to sink my teeth into his flesh right there. But there was no one here to put on a show for, and if we started crossing the line in this room, nothing would ever be the same. I brushed over the spot instead, willing it to be enough.

He stilled under my hand—the air charged and snapping with energy—while I glided the pad of my index finger over the ridge.

Our ragged breathing echoed between us—or maybe it was mine—and my gaze dropped to find his chest rising and falling just as predominantly as mine. God, but he was beautiful.

I saw a lot of different bodies day in and day out, but his was an almost a primitive masterpiece in a time when it had become common for people to modify their bodies in one way or another. No tattoos, no piercings, just one hundred percent natural man confident in his body. A surprisingly strong body considering his corporate job.

I bit my lip and forced myself to concentrate. Nudging his chin up and at an angle, I set the blade against his skin once more.

Scccrrrraaaaaaape.

The ringing in my ears almost obliterated the sound of the razor entirely. And there, under the bare strip of skin, I spotted the pulse point in his throat. His heartbeat fluttered under his skin. Such a vulnerable part of him, visible on the outside.

He leaned into me, his abdomen and all sexy parts south digging into the vanity now with a grunt. His hand slid around the outside of my thigh, no longer holding me still, but gripping me in a whole new way, keeping me anchored to his hip.

My hand shook ever so slightly as I brought the razor up again.

Scccrrrraaaaaaape.

Sweet baby Jesus, he smelled good. Like fresh sage and sea salt clinging to damp fresh skin. My face grew hot. The blood rushed into my cheeks, and I knew if I looked in the mirror, I'd look thoroughly fucked.

When he'd barely even touched me.

My eyes drifted shut as I clenched, doing anything possible to relieve this ache that started as a deep throbbing in my core but now flared at every pulse point from head to toe.

A low groan rumbled from his throat that had me glancing down to find my thighs squeezing him.

He tangled his fingers with mine and took the razor from my hand. "That's good," he said in a raspy voice I'd never heard before.

But it wasn't.

He only had half a shave.

I'd surrendered half of my resolve.

And we had a whole new craving brewing between us.

11
Charlie

I shoved the angels in my bag and waited for Nick to get dressed. They felt private like they were a part of me I wasn't ready to share with anyone. I hadn't figured out how I was going to get out of here for half the day tomorrow to shop if I didn't fess up, but I'd figure that part out later.

When he finally emerged, he wore a heart-palpitatingly sexy pair of faded blue jeans and a fisherman knit sweater pushed up to just below his elbows. I stared stupidly at the veins running along his forearms while he mumbled something about agreeing to meet our fathers at some new brewery in town. Since I hated beer, he figured we'd get a break from being on.

I should have been thankful, but instead, I spent an hour running his tone of voice and the expression on his face through my mind. I'd seen this look before. Before playoff-making games in high school. While he waited for grades on exams to roll in. Before and after his SATs.

Okay, we were both being stupid. So I shaved him. It wasn't like he shaved my lady bits or anything. It was a neck.

A harmless, edible neck.

Launching myself off the bed, I paced the room. I couldn't stay here, and the urge to ski fled when my libido climbed on a space shuttle to the freaking moon.

But there was something I could do that would bring this all back into perspective. I could see if my mom wanted to have lunch. Just a dose of reality—okay, more like a sledgehammer to the face, heaping of reality, but whatever helped me shake this lingering feeling in my stomach. Like pitching over the first hill on a roller coaster and finally catching my breath just to be pitched over again.

I found her and Mrs. McAdams coming out of the spa which was a total score for me. A morning being pampered might work wonders for the icy attitude of a certain saint's mother.

She clasped my arms and pulled me in for some sort of weird public hug thing she had started doing. Like she was afraid to show anyone that she had real affection for her kids. Or had at one time. Like when I was eight. "Charlie, dear. I'm surprised you're not on the mountain." She looked past my shoulder and searched the lobby behind me. "Where's Nick?"

Mrs. McAdams perked up then, her laser focus on me like my answer might come in code, harboring secrets or some shit.

"He met Dad and his father at some brewery that just opened. He'll be along later."

"Oh, that's too bad, I just love seeing you two

together looking so happy." Her smile widened and looked even genuine. "Settled."

"Easy, Mom. It's not like he put a ring on it. Don't put pressure on it, okay?"

"Of course not, dear. Come on, you look famished. Why don't we get you an order of that loaded baked potato soup you love."

See, getting a thorough rubdown by some hot masseuse named Emil worked wonders on a personality. "Sounds great." I turned to Nick's mother, smiled, and tried to ignore the collection of chilly expressions she'd aimed my way. "Will you join us, Mrs. McAdams? We'd love to have you."

Totally not true, but I figured I'd get a taste of the high road. Frankly, it tasted like shitty beer. Or a swig of orange juice right after brushing your teeth. And still, I plastered a smile on my face. Nick was doing me a favor and sure, there were perks in it for him too, but I never thought doing this might shove a wedge between mother and son. No matter what I thought of either of our moms, I didn't want to destroy lives here. I just wanted to enjoy the time I had without fending off the ex from hell.

She made a show of checking her watch.

"Your hair appointment isn't for another hour, Ellen," my mother said, linking arms with her best friend. "You've got time."

Ellen nodded, her mouth pinched.

Yup, reality just came skidding in, and I felt more balanced already.

We settled into a corner booth at the Rockport, one of the three restaurants in the lodge. We placed our orders, this time with no commentary from my mother. *Thank you, Nick.*

Potato two days in a row… see, a saint, likely with a direct line to God himself.

My mom's enthusiasm and Nick's mom's almost easy acquiescence had me a wee bit drunk on the power to maybe not move mountains, but nudge them a little.

Welp, intoxication was a fickle bitch and the first thing it did was jam my radar. So naturally, three bites in, drunk on fresh bacon crumbles, Nick's mom struck.

"So, tell me, Charlie… how long have you and my son been seeing each other?"

Oooof, nothing wrong with Nick's mom's radar at all. Maybe someone should get her a drink or anything over two hundred calories even, so we could be on an even playing field here.

I took a moment, pretending to chew potato while my brain scrambled for an answer. It had to be long enough that it didn't look bad that we shared a room but not so long we looked like we were hiding it. "About three months now," I said, keeping the answer fluid enough that I didn't have to point out an exact date for our relationship. Three months sounded about right, but also dangerous. A lot can happen in three months, and Nick and I weren't exactly close.

"Three months, you say? That's odd."

Oh shit.

"We ran into him on a dinner date not quite two

months ago. A beautiful woman," she said with a hopeful, yet spiteful lilt in her voice. "A touch too young, which is probably why it didn't work out, but still, according to you, you were dating him then."

My mother took a keen interest in me all of a sudden and two sets of perceptive eyes bored holes in my skull while they waited for a reply.

And only one explanation came to mind. "We were in an open relationship then." Oh my God… why did I say it like that? I could have just said we weren't exclusive. The term *open relationship* meant something else entirely and judging by their twin surprised expressions, they knew it.

Mrs. McAdams shook her head, her nose in the hair ever so slightly. "That doesn't sound like my Nicholas."

"How would you know? Have you dated him?"

Motherfucker.

My polite facade lasted all of twenty minutes.

"Charlotte Elizabeth!"

Well motherfucker again.

My mom middle-naming me in public was rare and it meant real trouble. "Would you excuse me for a moment?" In my hurry to get out of my chair, the leg dragging on the floor let out a horrendous scraping sound making me flinch.

I power walked to the bathroom, and the minute I made it out of sight, I called Nick.

"Hey, Trouble," he answered.

Trouble? If he only knew. "May-fucking-day, Nicky boy."

"Jesus, are you drunk already?"

"Nope. I just put my whole-ass foot in my mouth, and I'm hiding in the bathroom. You gotta get me out of this," I whisper yelled into the phone.

I heard a rustle on the other end as he told our fathers it was a client and he needed to take the call. My father's slightly buzzed voice came through the receiver. "Of course. I admire your work ethic, son."

A sigh of impatience slipped from my lips as I pressed my forehead against the cool door. "Can you please peel my father's lips from your puckered hole and help me out here?"

"Gross, Charlie," he said as the noise of the brewery faded, and the sound of cars grew louder.

"Well, if you think that's gross, you're not going to like anything I say next. Are you leaving?"

"Yeah."

"Do they have a ride? I don't want to add our father's deaths to my conscience."

"Dad said they'll get a car when they're ready to leave. Now, spill it. What did you do?"

Here goes nothing. "I thought I would do something nice—er—fine, normal and go to lunch with our mothers."

"And?"

It should be like ripping off a Band-Aid, one yank and it's over. But no, like with real Band-Aids, I peeled the edge back, wincing the entire time. "Your mom asked me how long we've been dating."

"Okay, not exactly the end of the world."

"You don't think so? Well, big problem, Nick. I said three months. Only your parents ran into you on a date *two* months ago."

"Shit."

"Yeah, and your mom decided to rub it in how beautiful your date was, Nick. That was fun. So naturally she wanted an explanation."

I heard the familiar sound of his car door closing and his engine firing up. "So what did you say?"

"That we were in an open relationship."

"What?!?!"

"I know," I hissed. "I panicked."

"Okay, we can fix this."

"We probably could have if…"

"If what, Charlie? How can there possibly be more?" His voice got deeper with every reply. Deeper, more sinister… the same thing in this case.

"Listen, before I tell you, I want it on record that I tried. I really did. I made the effort with them and attempted to thaw your mother out."

"Fine, you get credit for that, but spill it, Charlie. What did you do?"

"I might have more than thawed your mother out if the steam coming from her ears was any indication. She said an open relationship didn't sound like you so I…"

He hit the gas even harder, the sound of the engine revving and switching gears getting louder in the background. "Say it."

"I asked her how she would know; has she dated

you?" I flinched, waiting for him to give me shit, but all I got was silence.

Followed by an even louder silence.

"Nick? Are you there?"

"I swear, woman…" Oof, that was the voice… the potato voice from last night. "Your mouth is going to spark the end of the world one day."

"Maybe this is a good thing."

"Come again?"

"What I flipped the script so much that she'll be afraid to ask us anything else."

"You're not that lucky."

"But you are, and we're a team."

He let out a snort. "I'm not sure my luck is enough to save us from you."

"Guy, I'm sitting in a stall here. I'm going to need you to come up with a plan. How far away are you?"

"Five minutes. You're going to go back out there and tell them that I came back early from the brewery because I wasn't feeling well."

"Okay, and then what?"

"Then we're going to spend the rest of the day hiding in our room. If my mother thinks I'm under the weather enough that I'm actually going back to bed, she won't bring it back up."

"What if she tells your dad and your dad tells her you left to handle a client call."

"I'll say I got sick after."

"What if she wants to check on you."

"I'll tell her you're taking care of me."

"What if—"

"Charlie!"

"Okay… this is good. We can totally do this." I whipped open the stall door, making the woman washing her hands jump. "Sorry," I mumbled to her as I passed.

I hesitated just outside of the ladies' room. "Hey, Nick?"

"Yeah?"

"What about my soup?"

He growled. Like actually growled over the line. "Chaaarrrlllieee," he said, dragging my name out the same way I seemed to have stretched out the last of his patience.

"Look, it's damn good soup, and I was actually enjoying it without commentary from my mother, thank you very much."

"I'll buy you all the soup you want. I'll get it delivered by the bucketful if that's what it takes," he said with an exasperated huff. "Just get out there and extricate yourself from the mess you made."

12
NICK

"Okay, I see now. I get the concern about the soup." I moaned around another warm, thick bite. The flavor combinations of potato, cheese, bacon, and green onions burst in my mouth, and my stomach rumbled in demand for more. For a few minutes, our situation felt almost normal. If you didn't count the fact we were currently hiding in our room, sitting on the floor, our shoes kicked off, with our backs to the bed, *The Proposal* on the TV, devouring room service.

Making my escape earlier created a mess when Charlie was left to her own devices, but it saved us both from something a whole lot more terrifying than our parents finding out about our lie.

Turning our lie into truth.

Everything had become way too serious in that bathroom. We lost ourselves there and shifted into some alternate universe. Our antagonistic relationship slipped away every minute we spent as a couple, but into what? We weren't exactly friends.

Our ruse last night thrust me into this weird

unknown zone where I had no idea what was too far and what fell short when it came to selling this relationship to our families.

I'd forgotten about Mariah lurking entirely and my world narrowed down to one singular focus… Charlie.

I didn't know what it meant, but something—it definitely meant something.

All I had to do was pull out her chair, occasionally hold her hand, and lead her into the room with a hand to her lower back, my ass.

Charlie and I started tiptoeing over some important lines in less than twenty-four hours together. Anything that happened to us, between us—happened to our families and my best friend too—leaving us navigating a series of delicate dances.

Daniel putting his hands on her caused something inside me to snap—something I was powerless to fix. My head hadn't stopped agonizing over all the ways he touched her—picturing it even—leaving my blood boiling. It led to me imagining all the other ways he touched her, and nothing could scrub those images from my mind now. Once I smoked him the third time down that trail, I had nowhere to put that simmering agitation. Carrying it into our room and having her show up when she did turned that energy into something else entirely.

I'd never let a woman shave me. The thought never crossed my mind. And now it's all I could think about. Her scent—lavender and mint—surrounded me. Warm, thick thighs wrapped around my hips. The strangled catch of her breathing with every swipe of the blade.

The way she abandoned the razor and touched me —like she was helpless to resist.

The hard-on was swift, and the need destroyed my ability to analyze all the ways this could go terribly wrong.

I still ached—a state I figured I better get used to for the duration.

"Sorry about ruining lunch with our dads."

I glanced at her, the way she dragged the spoon out of her mouth upside down, her gaze on the TV completely oblivious to the thoughts pummeling me. How did she do that?

At least I could handle my dad. He didn't have any new material. Annoying. Frustrating. But familiar.

Tasting Charlie's mouth. Intoxicating.

My body wanted her. My brain was starting to waffle too. Telling me I could indulge, just for now, then walk away. We could leave everything we did with each other on this trip here at this resort.

I yanked my thoughts back into the present. Dads. She mentioned our dads.

"It's probably a good thing. One beer in and my dad started about how he always hoped his boy would take over the company. The beer was good, but not suffer through another guilt trip good." It didn't matter how I phrased it or how many times I said it, he just could not accept that I wanted nothing to do with running the business he built. He didn't take over his father's ad agency—something his father built and very much wanted my dad to run one day.

My father followed his own dream. He built his own legacy from the ground up. What he hadn't figured out was it could still be his legacy even if it didn't stay in the immediate family. He, more than anyone, should understand my need to forge my own path on my terms.

Besides, I wasn't his only option. Holly had shown interest time and again, but our father overlooked her to the point she gave up, and look at her now—accumulating enough college credits to technically qualify for a degree if she actually focused on a single course of study.

Instead, she traveled the world through travel abroad programs at her university on our parents' dime, almost in a holding pattern waiting for them to notice her—and accept her dreams.

Charlie shook her head next to me and let out an easy laugh. "How did we all turn out so much different than our parents?"

"Evolution?"

"It's more than that. Eve is a carpenter with spiked hair spending her free time playing roller derby. Chance committed to spending the next twenty years in the military. Your sister Holly is—" Her eyebrows snapped together. "What is Holly?"

"Other than a pain in the ass?"

She nudged me with her shoulder and smiled. "She's your little sister; she's supposed to be a pain in the ass."

"Yeah, well, luckily I'd learned some skills with little sisters before I had to deal with anything she threw at me."

"Yeah, who was that?"

"Funny, spawn."

"I don't know what you're talking about…" she said with a jut of her chin. "I'm charming."

"About as charming as a cobra," I muttered with a snort, putting us firmly back in Charlie and Nick territory. A place where the band around my chest loosened so I could finally take a full breath.

"But really, why are we so different than them? Haven't you ever wondered?"

I chewed, thinking about our parents, about these trips leading up to Christmas every year when other families had large gatherings with aunts, uncles, cousins, and… well damn. "They're only children."

She swung a confused look in my direction. "Huh?"

"Both of our mothers and fathers are only children." The realization hit me for the first time that our families weren't the norm. Maybe the fact that we hadn't realized until now said something. They gave us grief. They applied pressure every chance they got, but in their own way, they also tried to make sure we weren't alone. "All the expectations were heaped on them, and they grew up in a time where you didn't really break away from expectation. Besides, my dad, who seems to forget he did the exact thing he's disappointed in me for doing."

"Okay, that actually makes sense. Can you imagine what it was like for them growing up? Sounds lonely," she said, her voice getting quiet, almost introspective.

"We had no aunts and uncles, no cousins…"

"But they made sure we had each other." She dropped the spoon in her empty dish and set it aside.

"In their own way, they gave us an extended family the only way they could."

Chance was my best friend, but more than that, he was the brother I never had. Eve had honorary sister status despite my razzing Chance about fucking her. And Charlie… I looked at her then, taking in the tilt of her chin, the smile on her full lips—Charlie was just… different. More.

There was that pressure in my chest again.

She shot upright and snapped her fingers. "That's where we went wrong," Charlie said, nodding toward the TV. "No binder."

Grasping at another sliver of normalcy provided by her reaction, I glanced up at Ryan Reynolds and Sandra Bullock quizzing each other on the plane. "We grew up together… we shouldn't need a binder." The words sounded oddly like a grumble as I processed this new perspective… or maybe it had been there the whole time and I only just realized it.

"I could have used a binder to prepare me for lunch."

"A muzzle would have been just as effective."

She elbowed me then, completely unaware of the unease filling me. "You were off preparing to get schnockered, and I was in the trenches taking grenades. Grenades mind you, your mother pulled all the pins on."

Yeah, and she and I would be having a talk about

that. I gave her grace for the first night after Charlie pointed out her less-than-stellar reaction to our couple status, but only because we blindsided her. This was Charlie, her best friend's daughter; she had no reason to be giving her the cold shoulder. Not like this.

I'd never seen this side of her… or maybe I wasn't paying attention. Well, I was watching now and her behavior toward Charlie would stop. Tolerating it only meant she'd be emboldened to do it again with anyone I dated in the future.

Glancing at Charlie, my gaze traveled over the wisps of hair breaking free from her messy ponytail. Helpless to look away, I studied the way they moved when she laughed, the light brush tickling her pink cheeks until she flicked them out of the way, only to have them settle against her skin once again.

Anyone I dated in the future...

At least that's why I told myself I would set my mother straight. Only, sitting here, unable to tear my eyes from Charlie's profile, I could only see one future. And I had a bad feeling in the process of lying to our parents, I'd also begun lying to myself.

13

Charlie

"**W**hat's this?" Nick asked, his pinky catching the edge of the bag of angels I'd shoved under the bed skirt.

My heart jumped into my throat, and I snatched the bag away, tossing it in the corner. "It's nothing. Just a project."

"Those were angels from the tree downstairs." He'd gone still, his eyes shot open wide, his unwavering stare locked on me.

Goosebumps rose on my skin and embarrassment flooded my cheeks. Here we sat with a collection of sex toys pretty much looming right over us from where they hung on the bathroom door, but this… this was what was going to push me over the edge. "A few. It's nothing."

He shot to his feet, rounded the bed, snagged the bag, and peered inside. "The bag is full, Charlie."

"Your point?" God, couldn't he just drop it? I needed him to drop it. I was not ready for his reaction. Would he laugh? Worse, would he say nothing and not care at all? Indifference from Saint Nick, well, that might kill me. Despite the fact it never crossed my mind until this moment, I was painfully aware I'd never seen him go near the tree either.

"Every year you take off for a day," he said quietly. "Is this what you do? You shop for these kids?"

I put every bit of attitude I could muster in my cocked hip and crossed my arms, just daring him to poke at me about this. I'd punch him straight in the dick if he got out of pocket even once. "Yes, so what?"

"This has to be thousands of dollars' worth of presents."

"Nick, we all know you can math. Hell, you can math better than anyone I know. What is your point?"

"How do you afford this?"

I looked for any hint of suspicion in his voice—of judgment—but came up with nothing. I'd never seen this version of Nick before, and it left me with no clue as to how to handle the terrain of this conversation. "Ummm, it's called a job."

"And you make enough money to afford this?"

It took everything in me to not squirm. "Yes, but I also make sacrifices so I can afford that. Now can you drop it?"

"No."

My arms fell to my sides, and my mouth fell open. "Come again?"

"This is… this is selfless."

"Why the hell do you sound so surprised?"

He cleared his throat, and when he spoke, his voice came out low and if I didn't know better, full of wonder.

"Just processing… it's a lot." He grabbed an angel out of the bag and shot me a questioning glance. "An Xbox?"

"There are a few of them in there. I figured more bang for the buck if it's a gift for the family."

"Why haven't you said anything? Your parents would be pr—"

"My parents don't give a shit about the tree." The words flew out in a rush. He hadn't stopped staring at me. I couldn't even be sure he blinked. I'd kill for the split second safety of one blink. "Besides, I don't do it for praise. I do it for them," I said, gesturing toward the bag still tight in Nick's grip.

With measured movements, he set the bag down on the bed, his back to me. The seconds ticked by, the feeling of being trapped inside these walls with him for the rest of the day inciting full-blown panic blooming in my chest.

I could handle his clapbacks and needling me just as hard as I did him, but this pensive part of him had me ready to run. His stillness sparked growing turmoil in me I was helpless to control.

This was a mistake. All of it. We were so off our axis we'd never get back to where we began. A terrible foreboding washed through me at the risk of losing who we were to one another for an outrageous lie.

We needed to put a stop to this. I forced my feet to move. "Nick," I said quietly, curling my hand around his forearm. I had every intention of looking him straight in the eye while I called it all off.

His muscles tensed under my fingers, and before I could so much as blink, he rounded on me. The bag of angels falling to the floor, scattering next to us.

Whatever I intended to say died in my throat the minute he buried his fingers in my hair and tipped my head back impossibly far.

Giving up the charade became impossible the minute his mouth took mine, and he robbed the very breath from my lungs.

The kiss burned straight to my toes. His warm lips taking whatever he damn well pleased from me, he single-handedly catapulted us into a terrifying yet exhilarating reality.

My back met the wall, but I had no recollection of moving. My heart thundered in my ears, the rapid beat competing for attention with the sounds we made as we scrambled for more.

I met him stroke for stroke. Might have even managed the upper hand until he slanted his mouth and did some sort of magnificent swirl and swipe with his tongue and my knees gave out entirely. Never one to let anyone fall, he was there, both hands grasping my ass and lifting me right off my feet. My legs, the little hussies, screamed hallelujah and clamped right onto his hips.

Hard and demanding, he dug his hips into mine leaving very little to the imagination about just how much he packed behind his zipper and his ability to use it.

This moment gave me the chance to do what I'd

been fantasizing to since the minute I saw him get out of his car. Holding his face in my palms, I ran my thumbs over the soft hair of his beard, eliciting a jagged groan from him. My logical side, despite being a fraction of the size of my throw caution to the wind, screamed at me to stop this, but my body and heart stopped listening the minute he touched me.

Or maybe the minute I touched him.

Tearing his mouth free, he rested his forehead against mine, our lungs heaving and breath mingling between us.

My lips ached.

My body sang.

"I'm proud of you," he whispered over my lips.

And with four little words… my heart went all in.

14
Charlie

Nick's kiss packed more punch than an exorcism.

Four hours had passed since he let me slide down the length of him before letting me go.

Four hours of him going back to normal like he hadn't just yanked my spirit right out of my body.

He informed me he'd be going with me tomorrow to shop for the kids.

He ordered us dinner.

He bought two movies.

And he acted painfully… normal.

Every moment he continued on like our ruse hadn't spiraled into madness was a moment I contemplated all the ways I'd make him pay for the roller coaster he single-handedly strapped me into.

Now what? Are we kissing now whenever? Are we back to this being a show for the parents and in private we're… the old us?

Well, not really the old us, but us with a tentative truce.

Well, screw him and his truce when I still tasted him,

felt the burn from his beard lingering on my skin, and destroyed a pair of underwear when my body went up in flames during that kiss. A pair of underwear I still hadn't gotten a chance to change out of because there was no way I'd let him see what he'd done to me.

I glared down at him where he lay propped on his elbow, popping popcorn in his mouth while he laughed at something on the TV.

I should have shaved his beard clean off. All of it. And his head.

Frustrated, confused, and doing anything possible to avoid committing murder, I texted Eve.

ME
I hate him.

The wavy dots popped up on the screen, and I let out a sigh of relief.

EVE
Who?

ME
Who do you think? Nick.

EVE
Figures. What did he do this time?

ME
He kissed me, the shithead.

EVE
WHAT?????

ME

And get this... he told me he's proud of me.

EVE

So what are we talking here? A kiss on the cheek?

ME

The man kissed me so freaking hard and deep he romanced my cervix.

EVE

I could have done without that visual. In what damn universe are you and Nick kissing?

ME

I guess Mom didn't tell you.

EVE

Tell me what?

ME

That we're a couple now.

EVE

Wait—hold up. Did Mom put you up to this so I don't miss the ski trip next year?

ME

Not everything is about you, Eve. We're pretending so our mom and his mom will stop trying to hook us up.

EVE

Huh? But why would they hook you up if you're already hooked up?

ME

With other people. Not each other. They brought plus ones for each of us.

EVE

Ohhhhh, gross. So wait, if you're pretending to be a couple, kissing is part of it, no?

ME

It was in our room. No witnesses.

EVE

You're sharing a room?

ME

Chance didn't tell you?

EVE

Chance knows?!?!

ME

That we're roomies, not that we're a couple.

EVE

So you are a couple...

ME

Pretending to be. Are you drunk?

EVE

No, but after this conversation, I'll need to be.

ME

Forget I said anything.

EVE

Not fucking likely. Is he a good kisser?

ME

Not the point.

EVE

He's your fake boyfriend but kissing you off the clock, and now you're freaking out. It's the ONLY point.

ME

I hate you.

EVE

So he is a good kisser.

ME

I didn't say that.

EVE

Hate to break it to you, but yeah, you kinda did.

ME

Whatever. So what do I do now?

EVE

What are your instincts telling you?

ME

To smother him in his sleep.

EVE

Bad plan... orange is not your color.

ME

Prison uniforms are light blue in Maine.

EVE

Why do you know this?

ME

I looked it up the last time I didn't think I'd resist killing him.

EVE

Of course you did. If you want me to be the maid of honor, don't expect me in a dress.

ME

Bite me.

Less than an hour later, Nick lay fast asleep next to me, this time in a pair of gray sweats.

Only gray sweats.

A decision I considered a direct assault on my sanity.

Well, fine. Two could play that game.

I rushed through my nightly routine of washing my face, brushing my teeth, and braiding my hair. Tiptoeing around to Nick's side of the bed, I leaned over and poked his arm.

Nothing.

I poked harder this time… just to be sure.

Nothing.

I couldn't stop the devious grin. He thought the crotch rocket was bad? He'd be begging for amateur hour level humiliation after this.

Since I couldn't really kill him, I'd have to settle for practicing for his wake. Since we're currently a couple, I guess that meant it was up to me to design his send-off.

One by one I slid the dildos, butt plugs, nipple clamps, and bottles of lube from the garment bag. I laid them out in categories and then lined them up by length. And would you look at that, I had one dildo longer than all the rest, and it would be perfect right about there.

I laid the nine-inch lifelike cock on the available section of pillow directly over his head.

I always said Saint Nick was a unicorn of a man… and now he has his very own horn.

I grabbed my phone to memorialize the moment, careful to make sure the flash was off. I then grabbed the rabbit vibrator with the fancy little addition designed to tickle the skittle and the double dildo with a standard length and an extra mini dick in the perfect back door size. Those lay at a forty-five-degree angle, the smallest appendages aimed inward with the curve of the toy.

And just like that, the unicorn became the devil. I snapped another photo biting my lip to the point of drawing blood so I didn't burst out laughing and wake him up.

I continued on until I outlined his entire body with various toys in a kaleidoscope of colors.

One hand rested on his thigh, the other settled across his stomach, and right there, just above his hand was the perfect place for the three butt plugs.

I arranged them almost as though he held them like a bouquet, freezing when two knocked together making a clanking sound that seemed abnormally loud in the quiet room. Easing away from the bed, I went to take another picture but lowered my phone when I noticed a perfect spot for the mega wand he'd snuggled the night before.

The weight of the toy and the narrow space between his legs made placement precarious, but with a whole lot of patience, I managed to lay the wand right between his legs without touching his leg on the other side.

Kind of like playing Operation.

I snapped at least a dozen photos from multiple angles before dismantling my handiwork, putting all the toys away, and crawling under the covers. Grinning into the darkness, I choked on a laugh loud enough that it stirred Nick.

The laugh turned into a horny groan when he rolled onto his side toward me, wrapping his arm around my stomach. His fingers slipped under the waistband of my pajama pants and underwear just far enough to have me holding my breath. With one last adjustment, he nestled his erection right between my ass cheeks, sending my imagination spiraling out of control, leaving me staring into the night, incapable of so much as blinking.

15
NICK

CHANCE

EXPLAIN.

My eyes sank shut after catching a preview of the images Chance sent my way.

Just breathe. You will not kill her. It's fine. It's just a joke. Just more of Charlie being Charlie. At least this time she didn't take your crotches.

One eye cracked open, my distorted gaze landing on my jeans. Intact.

I clicked the first image. A second later, the image filled the screen, and a growl vibrated through me.

It was one kiss.

Okay, it was the kind of kiss that changed everything. But maybe not. We could just pretend it didn't happen. Or pass it off as getting swept up in the act for our parents even in private. We'd call it practice. That sounded good… just more practice.

Bullshit.

Nothing about pinning her against the wall and taking the opportunity to get my hands on that very

133

round, immensely soft ass was an accident. I knew it…
and judging by the evidence of her revenge on my
phone, she knew it too.

This changed everything.

ME

> Your sister is an evil, EVIL woman.

CHANCE

Where the hell did all the sex toys come
from?

ME

> It's her collection. She's pretty damn
> proud of it.

CHANCE

Level with me, man… are you two
hooking up?

CHANCE

I hate you for even making me ask
that.

That right there was the other part of this scaring
the hell out of me right now. Chance was going to hate
me for this.

But not if I stop at the one private kiss.

Dammit!

I was almost one hundred percent sure we weren't
stopping at one.

CHANCE

I definitely puked in my mouth a little.

I'd take grossed out over betrayal. Grossed out would pass.

It took every ounce of willpower I possessed last night to play it off like the kiss never happened long enough to sit through dinner and two movies with her.

I barely kept up with the storyline while I lay in that bed, snacking on popcorn I couldn't taste, getting a crash course in Emmy award-winning acting.

CHANCE

I'm going to need an answer. Are you guys hooking up?

ME

No.

It was the truth. For now.

If he asked me again tomorrow, I had no idea what the answer would be. There was no way to get away from each other. With her needling me every chance she got and me constantly taking the bait, or falling asleep first in this case, it would come to a head at some point.

CHANCE

Look... I don't know what's going on, but my gut is screaming at me right now. I just—you're not just my best friend, you're my brother. I don't want whatever this is to change that.

I stared down at the words, having no clue what to say. I wouldn't lie to him. The truth was, everything started changing the minute Charlie looked at me and said those four words, "We need to talk."

When it came to the change Chance was so afraid of… that was up to us, wasn't it? No matter what happened between Charlie and me, we could choose to not let it change us.

My fingers shook as I typed out the only thing that made any sense for where we found ourselves in this moment.

ME

So we promise not to let it.

My message was a vague admission but noncommittal at the same time. Charlie's feelings were her own, and she hadn't clued me in on them yet. I only knew my feelings toward her were rapidly changing.

Dots waved on the screen and stopped.

No words came.

They waved again and again and again… and still, nothing.

Dropping to the bed, I willed him to just say whatever he was struggling to say. Give me some sign that we'd be good no matter what happened.

The wavy dots flashed once more.

I closed my eyes and counted the seconds ticking, waiting to find out just how strong of a bond we had.

My phone vibrated in my hand.

Taking a deep breath, I looked down and read my fate.

CHANCE

> Don't hurt her. She comes across as
> tough as nails, but under her armor is a
> soft heart. Don't break it.

Tension thrummed through my shoulders and neck, like rubber bands stretched impossibly far, ready to snap at any minute. I read his message again, positive I hadn't read it right, but the words never changed.

It was all the blessing I would get for now, and I'd take it. It gave me enough guilt-free room to figure out what the hell was happening between us and what it all meant.

I had no idea what to say, how to reassure him, because the truth was, I was balancing on the edge of a cliff here. Seeing her vulnerable in the wake of exposing her secret made me realize the majority of my hesitation came from wanting to protect her.

Even if that meant protecting her from me.

ME

> She means as much to me as she does
> to you.

CHANCE

> But it's different now, isn't it?

I typed out my reply and stared down at the words. Here goes nothing. There was no going back after I hit send.

ME

> It's different now.

I meant it when I said I wanted to go with her today, but judging by the way she hightailed it out of here so silently, she needed to do this on her own.

I told myself not to take it personally. This was as personal as it got for her and she wasn't ready to let me in..

Until yesterday, I'd never seen her blush. Not once. I'd seen her cheeks flush from alcohol, laughter, from huge smiles she was helpless to hold back. Her whole life she marched into a room the absolute picture of confidence, daring anyone to try to dull her shine.

At least, that's what I always saw.

But now… I spotted the dings in the armor Chance spoke of. The barbs she let slide in an effort to keep the peace, yet still living on her terms. Yesterday afternoon, I watched her self-confidence slide into self-consciousness, and with it, I met a whole new side of Charlie. A fascinating part. She was the one person in my life who would understand the pro bono work, and the need to help people who were the most vulnerable.

At our core, we were the same.

My gaze caught on the pictures again... I smiled. Selfless or not, she was so going to pay for this.

16
Charlie

I was not supposed to catch feelings—after all, this was all my idea—but that was exactly what was happening.

Nick's fault.

All of it.

For someone blindsided by our arrangement, he sure knew how to play the part with ease.

Because of course he did. Like I said, he's good at everything. Everything.

His reaction to any slight in my direction screamed, "She's mine" and every cell in my body noticed, from my clit to my freaking stupid heart.

Then jumping into script, offstage, he laid the single hottest kiss of my life on me, making me want things.

Add to that, he knocked me right in the heart when he made a call, waved a magic wand, sacrificed a goat or some shit so he could move mountains and match my donation before I even dropped off all the gifts I'd bought today.

If it were any other guy, I'd swear he was doing this

to torture the shit out of me, but this was Nick. Unassuming, kind to everyone, generous to a fault Nick.

He'd made the organizer of the drive promise not to say anything to me about his donation, but the organizer's little elf had worked out the details with Nick and of course, fell in love with him during the process. She couldn't contain herself and gushed about him for a full ten minutes with the most obnoxious stars in her eyes.

No doubt she was hearing wedding bells and doodling her married name on a piece of pink paper at this very minute, planning out how many babies they'd have.

She was that enamored.

Well, fuck her. She couldn't have him.

I loved him first, dammit.

In a platonic way, of course. How could I not? He'd been an annoying part of my life for forever. One more testosterone-wielding butthead to intimidate the boys I liked and be an all-around watchful eye. He and Chance starred in so many of my firsts. They taught me how to ride a two-wheeler. They took me fishing, hiking, and camping. Everything they did, for the most part, they invited me to do too.

I grew up shooting hoops with Nick, roasting marshmallows with him, and stealing the good tube every chance I got when we were out on the lake.

And he let me… every single time.

He'd been stitched into every part of my past, but what we were doing here in the present, it made me want for a whole different future.

This wasn't supposed to happen to us.

I needed distance.

Which was why I was in an outdoor hot tub, a blanket of stars in the inky sky overhead, with three guys from New York City.

Without Nick.

Hey, I stopped by the room and left him a note. Besides, it wasn't like I was cheating. Nick and I weren't real, and these guys were definitely not interested in the equipment I had.

The subtle hum of skiers and lifts drifting over from the mountain where night skiing was in full swing lulled me into a sense of peace. The warm bubbles lapping at my skin drew out the tension, bit by bit. The conversation and laughter with random strangers solidified the quicksand I'd been traversing for three days now.

In the short time I'd been out here, I'd gotten to know them. It only seemed right since we shared communal hot tub waters and all. Matt, Seth, and Seth's husband, Landon, owned a marketing firm in the city. They hightailed it to New England as a reward for a successful year firmly in the green.

Since Seth was a Maine native, they came here. From the way they hung so close to one another, I strongly suspected Seth and Landon had an open marriage, and Matt dabbled in some kinky adventures with them.

They seemed like the audacious types who could appreciate my collection upstairs.

And if I was right, their sexy plans might be a bust if

I couldn't work the twinge out of Matt's back he earned after a full day of black diamond runs.

"You've got a huge knot right here." I pressed down with the heel of my hand and rolled along the hard ball under his skin while I held his shoulder, keeping him as still as possible.

He groaned. "It hurts, but for the love of God, I'm begging you, don't stop."

"I bet that's not the first time you've moaned those words," I said with a laugh, eyeing Seth and Landon.

"Nope, it's not," Landon said, tipping back his beer. He sucked off the foam clinging to his upper lip, his heated gaze locked on Matt, the silent exchange with just eye contact alone like public foreplay and a precursor of the night to come. Seth dead-ass stared at Landon's profile, but not with jealousy. Nope. With full-blown arousal burning in his eyes.

Maybe they more than dabbled. I'd bet money Seth lived for watching Landon and Matt viciously fuck.

Lucky bastards.

I could use a vicious fuck right about now.

"Am I interrupting?" Nick's amused voice rumbled behind me.

Mother of God, one might argue this man's timing was pure perfection.

Any other man would have started with a jealous outburst first and asked questions later. But not Nick. That freaking halo. Sometimes it blinded the shit out of me.

I glanced over my shoulder. He stood there, a grin

tipping his lips, a pair of swim shorts slung low on his hips and a towel tossed over his shoulder.

My heart flipped over in my chest, a slow roll as I took every last inch of him in, knowing what he did today.

Don't fall in love with him. Don't fall in love with him. Don't fall in love with him.

"Hey." Oh God, that sounded breathless. Or maybe it was just me.

Matt glanced over his shoulder with an arched brow.

Okay, so not me. I totally sounded like a bitch in heat after gobbling up the view.

I just want a vicious fuck. That's it. *No feelings* I told myself as I scrambled to build a figurative wall of bricks around my heart.

"Hey," he said, leaning against the beam nearest to the tub. "Steppin' out on me?"

The hastily built jagged wall toppled over.

"I have a feeling you'd be welcome to join us," I said with a laugh, mentally stacking once again.

Matt sat on the lower step between my thighs while I pummeled the muscles in his back. Seth and Landon, well, they occasionally brushed against me as they started making out in the corner closest to me.

Matt hummed, his interested gaze snagging on Nick and traveling over him from top to bottom. "He's definitely invited. He yours?"

I scoffed. "It's complicated."

"It's really not," Nick answered with a lift of his brow. "I'm hers."

His tone left no room for argument, the sound setting off butterflies low in my belly. Two words and he had me knocked right back off-balance, even more so than this morning with Daniel.

"So, I'll just appreciate the view then," Matt practically hummed as his eyes roamed over Nick's bare chest.

And even Nick's reaction was pure perfection. His arms hung loosely at his sides. He made no effort to hide. He stood there, unbothered by the eye fuck Matt delivered.

The hot little MMM session in my head exploded into an inferno.

"What on earth!" My mother's shrill voice cut across my nerves and the butterflies fluttered to the pit of my stomach in an instant death, cooling my fevered blood and obliterating any buzz of arousal lingering in my veins.

Okay, so this looked bad.

Seth and Landon had settled right up against me, and I definitely hadn't noticed that Landon had reached around to find the front of Matt's shorts where he had a death grip on Matt's dick. And while I was watching Nick, I'd definitely gotten a bit overzealous with Matt. While I dug into the rigid muscles in his back, my other hand had crept up his chest to the base of his throat in a grip that looked positively possessive and like a promise of what was to come.

I definitely appeared to be stepping out on my man orgy style.

After telling Nick's mom we had an open relationship.

My mother, God love her, was actually standing there clutching a set of pearls around her throat.

Because of course she was.

Nick grinned, that smug smirk saying, how do you plan to explain this one?

Challenge accepted.

"What's going on here?" Nick's mother demanded from where she stood with my mom when no one spoke. Ironically, she was not clutching a set of pearls. Instead, she had her hands on her hips, her chest puffed out, ready to go to battle. No doubt she'd restocked her damn grenades.

A total mood... and one I had to respect despite having been on the receiving end of sharp daggers flying at me from narrowed eyes.

"It's no big deal. Nick's a cuck. He likes to watch."

Nick's mouth flattened into a grim line, and his eyes blazed with a furious intensity, promising revenge.

"A cuck? What's a cuck? Is this a sex thing?"

Matt glanced over at Seth and Landon, who'd stopped fucking each other with their tongues long enough to take in the show. They all burst out laughing and in unison said, "For everyone but the cuck."

"So, it is a sex thing," his mother said. "Nick, are you gay?"

"No, Mom, I'm not gay." He took each of their elbows and steered them back the way they'd come, but not before shooting a hot, hard look over his shoulder and mouthing the words, "You're dead."

17
NICK

Close proximity to Charlie was akin to being on a world record-holding thrill ride and simultaneously getting your fingernails ripped out one by one.

"What exactly is a cuck?" Mrs. McAllister asked in that wary tone of hers. She wanted to know, but definitely did not want to know.

Oh, I could not hate this conversation more. "It's a man who gets off on being degraded by watching his girlfriend or wife cheating on him with another man."

"And you like that?" My mother's shrill voice made me flinch.

"Mom, she was joking."

"So you're not gay or this cuck thing, right?" Her voice climbed a couple octaves, traveling far and wide through the lodge.

Heads swiveled in our direction, followed by barely restrained laughter. Charlie wasn't the only one taking grenades, and she was damn well going to hear about it.

"Jesus. Keep your voice down. No, I'm not gay or a

cuck. Those guys out there were gay and completely uninterested in Charlie, relax."

Leading our mothers through the common area, I prayed they'd stay silent until I found somewhere private to smooth this over.

I'd kill to be cleaning up the open relationship mess compared to this.

Snagging the semi-private room we'd had dinner in on the first night, I pulled out a chair for each of our mothers. It wasn't perfect, but it would have to do.

"This is going to kill your father, you know? First, you turn down the company, a decision no doubt a direct result of her influence."

I stared down at the woman I had admired for my entire life, the look on her face so unfamiliar, it knocked me off balance almost completely.

Who the hell was this woman and what did she do with my mother?

I drew on every bit of patience I could muster to keep myself from yelling at her for what would be the first time in my life.

Charlie's mom went stock-still for a full five seconds before she finally turned to glare at my mother. "Her influence? And what is wrong with her influence, Ellen?"

So that was Mrs. McAllister's line? Really? She poked at Charlie's food, her weight, the way she talked, her brazenness at every turn, and God knows a litany of other imagined transgressions, but my mother's perspective on Charlie's influence was going to be the thing that finally prompted her to speak up for her daughter?

My mom leaned in and slapped her hands on the table. "You said it yourself, Laurel, she's not serious about anything. Did you see her out there?" she said, pointing in the direction of the hot tubs. "Did you really take a good look? That's her job. Rubbing people for money. It's disgusting."

"You pay people to rub you every time you come here, and you prefer a very specific someone… Emil." My fingers turned white with how hard I strangled the back of the chair so I didn't strangle my own mother. "You don't seem to find that disgusting." I had so much to say, but I would bite back the words until she let it all out once and for all. Because this would be the only confrontation on this issue and her treatment of Charlie would change.

Her pinched expression met mine. "That's different."

"How?" I asked with a steely calm I didn't feel.

"The people I'm paying are not dating my son!"

My eyebrows shot up. She definitely didn't take notice of my tone and the warning it held. "Are you finished?"

I caught a glimpse of Mrs. McAllister, the way awareness filled her. The way her gaze frantically darted between us. Our exchange, and a completely different side of me she'd never been privy to, no doubt made her question the ways she treated her own daughter. Like a series of puzzle pieces sliding into place, the picture ugly and unfair, filling her with shame. A part of me, a furious part, hoped she choked on it.

"She's distracting you from a successful future. She's distracting you from someone who is right for you in every way."

And that was another whole problem, the crux of everything. My parents didn't see me as a success now. And they may never see me as a success as long as I refuse to follow in my dad's footsteps.

Bone-deep disappointment filled me, and I saw my mother with new eyes. She would rather see me tethered to Mariah and miserable than living a life full of adventure and loving, with someone who would make every day new and exciting.

No expectations. No maneuvering. Just pure acceptance.

Because despite being so different, in our hearts we were the same. And together, who knew what we could accomplish. What I only just now realized was the moment I spotted those angels in that bag was the moment I started wanting to find out.

After I punish the little shit, of course. No need to let her think she had the upper hand this early on. The delicate balance of our power dynamic would definitely set the foundation for a lifetime to come.

So yeah, she definitely had to pay.

"Just so we're clear, Mariah and I were never going to happen, with or without Charlie in the picture."

"But—"

"Never, Mom. She's manipulative and vindictive,

and I would think if you loved me, you'd want me to find someone who could actually love me the way I deserve. She's not it. She's not capable of it. She's never been capable of it."

"But the more time she spends with you, she'd learn—"

She said it so matter of factly, like pushing her son to commit to a lifetime tethered to someone he had to fix was just a minor inconvenience instead of a life-altering sentence. "Learn what? To be a decent human being? So what, I'm supposed to settle and then hope I can change her?"

She crossed her arms and huffed out an exasperated breath. "But you think you can change Charlie."

"That's what you don't get," I said quietly, "I don't want to change, Charlie." I stilled, the truth careening into my head and heart as the words settled between us, strong and resolute.

I turned to Mrs. McAllister then because if I looked at my mother for one more minute, I'd blow. "Your daughter doesn't want to embarrass you… so she swallows every snide insult you hurl at her, because that's who she is to the core. She'd spend a lifetime doing that so you never feel even a fraction of what you make her feel." I settled my palms on the table and leaned in, forcing her to look me in the eye and giving her nowhere to retreat. "Make sure she doesn't have to."

Mrs. McAllister nodded, and I was almost positive she got the severity of the message, but just in case…

"Charlie will protect you, but I won't. Not at her expense. I want you to remember that."

Her eyes glossed over with unshed tears and though it made me feel like all kinds of shit for speaking to her this way, I wouldn't stop until I made myself crystal clear. "If you ever make a comment about the food she eats, her weight, her profession—if you ever so much as make a face at her chosen nail color, I won't hesitate to call you on it no matter who is watching."

She gave me a jerky nod as the first tear fell down her cheek. I hated what I was doing to her, but I hated what she did to Charlie far more.

With a deep breath, I turned my attention back to my mother. I couldn't read the look in her eyes as she stared at her best friend, but I had to imagine this was the first time in their lives they stood in such stark difference to one another and in this moment, it left my mother with no backup.

"Make what you said in this room the last derogatory thing you ever say about, Charlie." My mother opened her mouth, and I sliced my hand through the air. "I mean it, Mom. I don't know where this is going. But I do know that if you blow my chances at something amazing, I will never forgive you for it."

I pushed myself upright and flexed my fingers at my sides. My shoulders ached, and my throat grew tighter with every word. "I'm walking away now before I say something I'll regret... but just so we're clear, I'm walking right back to Charlie because she's the only place I want to be."

18
NICK

Charlie was trying to kill me.

I couldn't prove it, but if this were a trial, a jury of all men would seal her fate.

"Charlie!" I half growled, half yelled her name as I barged into our room.

I'd marched our mothers through the fucking lobby in nothing but swim shorts, having to explain to both of our mothers with at least thirty people lurking, what cuckolds are.

Dropping hard truths and breaking their hearts was just the icing on the cake.

My hammering heart echoed in my ears, and blood pounded through my veins. My palms ached from clenching my fists for so hard and long.

Now she had to pay.

We were supposed to be a team on this.

By the time I'd returned to the hot tubs, she was gone. As near as I could tell, I was getting a glimpse of what an actual relationship with Charlie would be like. Practical jokes, misunderstandings, a lot of anger, and a constant state of horniness, all morphing into the singular desire to wrap my hands around that soft neck and choke the life right out of her.

My moral compass had a workout coming.

Spotting the closed bathroom door, I stalked over and pounded with the side of my fist. A cuckhold? Not a fucking chance. "Get your ass out here, spawn."

The sound of her muffled laugh broke through the red haze, followed by a loaded sigh. But it was the third sound reaching my ears that changed everything.

Buzzing.

That. Little. Shit.

"You better not be doing what I think you're doing."

"Be out in a few minutes!" she called, her voice grating on my every ball-aching nerve. The sound of the jets kicking on drowned out the sounds that followed, leaving me with nothing but my very vivid imagination and deprived, aching dick.

The fuck she would.

Saint Nick, my ass.

I grabbed my wallet and slid out the two bobby pins inside. The beauty of resorts like this tucked into nostalgic towns in the northeast? They liked to hold on to original aesthetics, focusing on restoration instead of modernization. It also meant I could be in that bathroom in under ten fucking seconds.

I stripped the rubber ends off with my teeth. With a couple of twists, I had the pins straightened and buried in the lock.

I may not have had older brothers to teach me this

kind of shit, but I had Chance. And Chance loved getting into places he didn't belong.

I would bet he never thought I'd be using the skills he taught me to barge in on his baby sister while she got off in our tub, but hindsight was a kick in the balls. At least for older brothers.

The lock caught, clicked, and released. My chest tightened. I sucked in a breath and threw open the door.

The tub stood on a two-tier platform just under a picture window with stunning views facing the west side of the mountain. Something I hadn't really paid much attention to at first, but now, the layout put her on display like an offering.

If I stood on that first step, right at the edge, I could tip her head back as far as she could possibly go and fuck her throat. The vivid image flashing in my mind propelled my feet, and in three strides, I was on the first tier and fuck my life, as I suspected, the perfect lineup.

She completely ignored my presence and continued to focus on her pleasure. Another part of her plan to drive me batshit crazy, no doubt.

And it worked.

Words died in my throat and all I could do was watch the scene before me, a live porno, but so much better, because it was Charlie—just Charlie—and all of the parts of her I'd never seen before.

Frothy water lapped over her breasts. Full and round, they rose and fell with her labored breathing. She pinched the one nipple and her lips parted on a gasp. Her other hand disappeared under the water. With her head thrown back and her eyes squeezed shut, her throat flexed as a strangled cry tore from her throat.

Goddamn.

My skin hot and tight, my muscles rigid, my cock harder than it had ever been—I stood there helpless to the feelings and want engulfing me.

Water sloshed as she bucked against her fingers. Rivulets spilled down her skin, catching on her tight nipples. Her lungs heaved with the power of her orgasm. Letting go of her nipple, she threw her arm back and gripped the edge of the tub. Bowing up, she sent more water rocking up the side, giving me a quick flash of her thighs flexing, her soft belly, and tattoos wrapping from her back around her ribs.

She better plan on more because she'd be doing this all over again.

On my watch.

Under my command.

Who was going to keep her from fucking me was the right question. Only, little did I know, the fucking came as everything she did *except* ride my cock. Fucking me was the wounded look she struggled to hide. It was her making light of our sleeping arrangements and making the setup so ridiculous that I slid into a deep sleep without agonizing over it. It came in the way she said fuck you to the showdown between Daniel and me and beat us both because she didn't need a man to fight her battles for her.

And it came in the way she studied me when she thought I was sleeping. Curious, soft eyes raking over every inch of my skin. Instead of the predictable heat of attraction, her perusal evoked quiet wonder and affection.

Between the soft and the spunk, I was about to break the code and fuck every bit of wildness right out of my best friend's little sister.

She better plan on a lifetime because I refuse to be without her, with this memory torturing my every waking moment for forever.

A pink flush flooded her cheeks, and she smiled as she glanced up at me. "Can I help you?"

Shoulders tight, cock aching, I loomed over her, burning with want. We'd get there, but first, "I just had to explain to our mothers what a cuck is."

"Bummer." Her tinkling laugh mocked me.

I had a powerful urge to not just bury my cock in that tempting throat but bury it so deep she choked on it.

"Meanwhile, you take off up here and decide it's playtime."

She scooped up a handful of water and ran it over the best tits I'd ever seen. "Seemed like a good idea at the time." She shrugged one shoulder. "I was frustrated."

"Frustrated? You were frustrated."

Her gaze snagged on the front of my shorts. With her eyes blazing, she bit her lip.

She wanted it. Good, because she was getting it.

"Frustration is cleaning up the messes you keep making with your smart mouth." I yanked the string of the waistband and forced them down my thighs until my cock sprang free.

Her eyes shot open wide, her mouth forming a little O of surprise.

I smirked down at her while I grasped my shaft and gave it a long, purposeful stroke.

"You want to talk about frustrated," I said, reaching for her hair and burying my fingers in the wet waves. Locking the strands in my fist, I tugged until a surprised gasp broke from her soon-to-be fucked throat.

"You've had me on the ragged edge from the minute you wiggled that round ass of yours against my dick in front of our parents. Then the kiss—"

"That kiss was all you, Saint—"

I yanked her head back. "Do I look like a fucking saint to you right now?"

Her eyes flashed and those straight white teeth sank into her plump bottom lip. Her hand crept between her legs to the bare pussy just under the surface of the water. "Do you think breaking in here and pulling my hair makes you anything else?"

I bent over her and pinched her jaw between my finger and thumb, hovering so close over her mouth, the puffs of breath panting from her lips wafted over mine.

"Breaking in and pulling your hair is only the beginning." With my eyes on her, I bit her bottom lip.

She gasped. From arousal or pain, I didn't know. I didn't care. When it broke free, I let her go and swiped the bite with my tongue.

Out of the corner of my eye, I spotted something

familiar. Beyond the ripple of water lay a hot-pink vibrator at the bottom of the tub between her those creamy, round thighs. "Seems like a shame to settle on just one when you have an arsenal."

"I'm limited on hands."

"Hmmm," I hummed over her mouth. "I can fix that, but first…" I ran my hand along the column of her neck, not letting myself go any farther. Pushing to my feet, I guided my cock to her mouth and ran the head along her plump lips. "Open, spawn."

Defiance blazed in her eyes, but she licked her lips and parted them anyway.

I hooked my thumb over her bottom lip and tugged. "You're going to have to open a lot wider than that."

When she did, my balls drew tighter, and I pulled her hair down even more, tipping her head back farther, stretching her throat open before sliding into the hot, wet cavern of her mouth.

Teeth scraped along the veins of my cock and I shivered, my eyes sinking closed, my hips aching to flex until I felt her throat bulge under my fingers from the invasion.

"You've done a lot of shit to me over the years, but the picture you sent Chance of me cuddling that fucking cunt rocket out there, and the one with me surrounded by your arsenal, those are the ones you're going to pay for, for years to come."

I thrust deep, and God fucking help me, her throat accepted me. She grabbed my ass, her nails sinking into my skin, the sting prompting my hips to buck, sending me deeper.

Her searing gaze never left my face, even as tears sprang to her eyes. She whimpered and squeezed her thighs together, her fingers clutching the edge of the tub until her knuckles turned white with the force.

Back bowing, she bucked. I retreated for a beat while she took a jagged gulp of air. Before she could get her bearings, I buried myself deep again.

"You should see the sight you make stretching around my cock. Beautiful." I grazed my fingers along her cheek. "That devious little mouth of yours so utterly destroyed never looked better."

A gleam of satisfaction burned in her eyes as she arched until she had both arms wrapped around my hips and the globes of my ass at the mercy of those biting claws.

With a rebellious glint in her watering eyes, she devoured me with her mouth and marked me with her nails until beads of sweat broke out along my spine. My body begged for release in the scorch of flames flowing under my skin.

And I wanted more.

Locking both hands on her throat, I closed my eyes and sucked in a painful gulp of air. "Do it again."

I focused on the rosy flush spreading over her breasts, coveting the tight nipples I planned to spend an obscene amount of time devouring.

Her nails caught on the previous scratches even as

they carved new ones. Helpless to stop the growl, I yanked free.

She smiled up at me as she swiped away the saliva running from the corners of her mouth. "If these are the consequences of those pictures, you better sleep with one eye open because I see so much more humiliation in your future."

"We'll see if you still feel that way when we're through. Out of the tub."

"Where are we going?"

"Wherever the hell I want, and right now, I want you out of the tub."

I kicked off my shorts and tossed her a towel. Leaving her there to dry off, I grabbed the garment bag off the door and threw it on the bed.

She watched me from the doorway as I laid a pillow down the center of the mattress and settled the wand along the length of it.

"What—"

"Get on the bed."

"Nick—"

My gaze snapped to hers. "Get on the fucking bed, Charlie."

She swallowed hard, no doubt choking back that pride, and undid the knot between her tits before sauntering over. All accentuated movements, the little shit tried to short-circuit my brain with a view of her ass and flashes of her glistening pussy as she crawled smack in the middle of the mattress, right behind the wand.

Ink carved along her spine and shoulders, lightning

jagged and sharp like veins threading under her skin, shooting in every direction.

A true representation of her if I ever saw one. Pure lightning. Loud, electric, powerful, unexpected, and fucking wondrous to watch.

"I'm disappointed, Charlie," I said taking a step toward her.

"So many options and accommodating holes, yet all you had in that tub with you was a simple pink vibrator." I dragged my fingertips over the clear plastic sleeves holding an array of toys in a variety of shapes, sizes, smooth, ridged—you name it, she had it.

"It got the job done," she said with a shrug.

"Did it? So you're completely satisfied? No part of you left wanting?"

"Sure." Her thighs squeezed again. It was subtle, but I saw it, and I knew she was a liar.

My eyes cut to the plugs in a row under the vibrators, the variety of lube, all promising unique pleasures.

And the clamps.

So many ways to use her body sitting unused.

Until now.

I took the nipple clamps out first and tested the tension. I assumed she'd already adjusted them to those tight little buds of hers. If I could take the ache of the broken skin on my ass, she could take more pain too. I twisted each of them a half turn, and she rewarded me with a sharp, surprised breath.

No doubt she thought I didn't know my way around her equipment.

Heat flared in her eyes as I reached for her, drawing my finger along one stiff peak. She swayed toward me and I clamped the first nipple, eliciting a shiver as pleasure zinged through her.

"You're a liar, spawn. Your mouth is all lies, but your face tells the truth. Your parted lips, the flush blooming over your creamy skin, the way you try in vain to soothe the ache between your legs… they've all conspired to reveal the little deceiver you are." Kissing her mouth, teasing her tongue with mine, I pinched the other nipple until she was whimpering and panting out my name in a needy whisper.

Another clamp snapped into place, drawing a sharp hiss.

I traced along her ribs, over the swell of her belly, and dipped my fingers between her legs.

Hot, drenched, and pulsing, her thighs flexed on me as I parted her impossibly wet pussy and sank two fingers as far as they'd go.

I ground my teeth as the ache in my balls ratcheted up several notches from the feel of her wet heat gripping my fingers. Pulling them free, I brought them to her lips and sent them deep… to the knuckle. With every tug of her tongue, I memorized her mouth, her mewling pleasure telling me just how much she liked the taste of her own pussy.

I wasn't just going to fuck Chance's little sister.

I was going to destroy the desire for any man beyond me.

19

NICK

"I bet you do this when you're alone. You can't reach that sweet pussy with your mouth, but you find a way to eat yourself, don't you, spawn?"

She tried to deny it past my fingers, but the challenge in her eyes gave her away. Wrenching free, I took her mouth hard and deep.

Musky and addicting, her flavor burst on my tongue, and I couldn't get enough. I wanted to devour every inch of her pussy clear to her ass. I wanted every hole filled up and her riding that fucking wand until she was a crying, convulsing mess in the center of this bed.

Ragged breaths and low, husky groans rumbled in her throat. I memorized every vibration, every sound as my craving for her, for dominance, grew.

This woman was *the only* woman who could stand toe to toe with the tension and energy colliding inside me. In this unfamiliar place, with so much hanging in the balance, I should be immobilized with fear, but no, apprehension settled into a sense of rightness making me push farther and want more.

Tearing my mouth from hers, I snatched the her

dirty bag of tricks and hauled it over to us. "How much can you take?" I traced over her bottom lip while she glanced down at the plugs.

Breathless and flushed, her lungs heaved as she stared hotly at my mouth. "How much do you want to give?"

All. I wanted her impossibly full. When reality hit us, when we were supposed to snap out of this arrangement, I wanted her to choose me... and this.

Because I had already chosen her.

"Everything."

Her eyes snapping to mine—searching—told me she knew I meant more than the physical, and we'd talk about it, but for now, I slid the biggest plug from the pocket. Cool glass sat heavy in my palm as I snatched the tingling lube from the sleeve. Resting the toy in her hand, I flipped open the cap and squeezed a generous amount into my cupped fingers.

With my nose buried along the edge of her neck, I savored the way she tipped her cheek against me, her body naturally curling into mine, wordlessly pulling me in even more.

Trailing my fingers over the crease of her ass, I dipped deeper, rubbing the thick liquid along her tight hole.

She jerked in my arms, but I supported her and held her steady, with her sultry gasp caressing my ear.

Every touch killed me bit by bit, washing away the Nick I was before we started down this road, leaving a new Nick in its wake. The one desperate to taste her, to fuck her, to keep her.

"You drive me insane, spawn. Everything you say, everything you do. You are the lightning, and fuck if I can't resist your strike." I sank my middle finger in her ass while tugging the cord of the nipple clamps. She cried out, her body bowing into me, her face turning into mine, where she slayed me with a deep, devouring kiss.

My pulse spiked as euphoria took over, and my heart swept away under powerful influence.

We each fought for the upper hand as our tongues tangled, our teeth gnashed, and I continued fucking her hole with my finger.

"Add another." Her voice cracked as she murmured the dirty request into my mouth.

She didn't have to tell me twice.

The minute I gave her what she wanted, she cried out, sinking down, driving me deeper, taking more, until she was quivering in my arms, with beads of sweat dotting her fevered skin.

I grasped her jaw and forced her face up to mine. Grey eyes shot with streaks of silver and glazed over in ecstasy stared unashamedly back at me.

"God, look at you," I rasped, my throat tight, my body absolutely on fire for her. "You were designed to look just like this. Flushed skin and so fucking soft," I let her jaw go then and traced along the damp column of her throat, my fingers buried in her tight ass giving her just enough to keep her focus on me. Just me.

She rose up and bit my lip with a hiss sliding almost completely off my fingers. "Lost in pleasure…" I murmured over her skin until I found her earlobe and caught it in my teeth. "And mine."

She snapped, the guttural sound from her throat a precursor to the show as she fucked herself mercilessly on my hand. Bracing with her palms on the mattress, her fingernails scored the cotton as she clenched the sheets in her fists. Her head fell forward, the air all but ripping from her lungs now and she pushed faster and harder.

And when she came, it tore through her with such force, she threw her head back sending wet locks of hair lashing along her inked back.

I should have known, should have been prepared for her to utterly destroy me this way.

My pulse pounded behind my eyes, every breath tearing its way out of my chest. I yanked my fingers free and stepped back, the abrupt loss causing her to fall forward on her hands.

I needed more.

"Turn around and put it in."

Still coming down from the high with damp ropes of hair framing her flushed face, she stared at me, her glazed eyes full of questions.

"Turn around so I can watch that plug stretch you wide before disappearing into that tight little asshole." I nudged the underside of her jaw and bit her chin. "Now."

The sheer look of awe on her face had me grinning.

Struck silent, she scrambled to do as I told her and bent down with her back arched until her nipples dragged over the sheets.

The head of my cock leaked as I stroked. I couldn't help but reach out and palm her ass while I settled in for the show. She brought the cool glass to her asshole and huffed out a series of tight breaths as she pushed it in farther and farther, slowly stretching that ring of muscle until her lungs heaved.

Just past the widest section, her body naturally drew the toy in, her asshole settling around the base, locking it in place.

My heartbeat pounded in my ears as my heart threatened to explode in my chest. I flicked the switch to the massive wand she still straddled, making it vibrate to life. "Now ride."

She reached for me, but I stepped away. I just wanted to watch her. Needed to watch her.

She growled, her hands fisted against the bed, making her look like a rabid little fox glaring up at me. "I swear to God if you don't fuck me—"

"I am fucking you. Just as brutally as you've fucked me with your antics since you could walk," I said. "Now squeeze those fucking thighs around that wand and ride, Charlie."

She craned her neck like she had to shake off the visceral instinct to defy me. But I waited her out and continued to stroke my cock, slowly, methodically, leaving no ridge untouched with each pass.

With her gaze locked on my movements, her body took over.

Settling over the wand, she adjusted, her fingers disappearing between her legs and parting that pretty pink pussy until she had the head nestled against just the right spot.

Her eyelids drifted shut and her hips rolled. Lips parting on a gasp, she disappeared into a haze of need, her hands moving over her own skin, teasing the cord between her tits, tugging her nipples before letting them snap back.

A low groan slipped from her lips.

"Talk to me, baby. Tell me how you feel."

"Full. Hot. God, I ache." A whimper escaped as she ground down against the vibrating head. "Nick, please…"

"Soon, baby. God, if you could see yourself right now… I'll never scrub this view of you from my mind." I fisted my cock harder, aching, but not quite at the edge of what I could take. "Keep rolling those gorgeous hips and haunt me forever."

She delighted in driving me to madness. Her brazen side, with a complete lack of shame, exuded such potent sexual power I had to fight the urge to drop to my knees in actual worship while watching her come apart for the second time.

An absolute expert in her own satisfaction, knew just how to pleasure herself completely. I'd never get enough of watching her like this.

A guttural cry that tore from her throat filled the

room. Her hips jerked in a jagged pattern as she clasped the wand and ground her clit against the head. With her head thrown back, she spasmed and shuddered, drowning in sensation.

Every move, every sound, the scent of sex surrounding us, it all carved itself into my memories, ensuring a lifetime of playing this moment over and over.

My throat ran dry and my palms itched to touch her. I forced myself to stay back, to stand on the outside of her orgasm as it shook her to the core.

Push and pull. All the time. In the smallest of ways, everything between us reduced to the fragile balance of opposing forces.

Snatching a condom from my grooming kit on the dresser, I made my way to the bed and settled in behind her. Her head fell back against my shoulder while I rolled on protection. I licked along her salty shoulder, the flavor of her damp skin tattooing itself on my tongue.

Everything had changed. We'd never be who we were to each other before.

I tucked my hand under her hair and gripped her neck, guiding her down until her face settled against the mattress. With her ass high in the air, the wand vibrated against her swollen clit. The jeweled base of the plug winked up at me. I gave it a firm tug, just enough to send sensation rippling through her, as I worked myself inside her.

"God, you're so full. I feel that glass filling that

fucking amazing ass. The way it drags along the side of my cock from the inside." I sank deeper, gritted my teeth, and squeezed my eyes shut as the orgasm I'd been staving off screamed for more. "Christ."

She let out a choked cry. "Nick! I can't—just do it. It's too much. I'm begging you. Please. I need to come again."

Gripping her ass, I dragged her up, her hips jutting in the air at a crude angle. "You can and you will do it," I said sinking the rest of the way in. "Trust me, spawn. I'm going to take care of you."

She yelped and despite the sound, ground back on me the way she did with my fingers, her hot pussy demanding more. I leaned over her and fisted her hair with my other palm curled around her hip. Dragging out of her tight heat, suspended with the tip sheathed in her soaking slit, I pumped back in hard and deep.

I set a punishing pace while I played with the plug. I tortured us both with careful strokes, almost settling fully into her and stopping, never quite letting her get as full as she wanted. When it became too much, and I finally plunged deep once again, the force made her buck.

Every time she lurched forward, I tugged on that gem between her cheeks, eliciting pleasure-filled cries. Cries turned to screams when her orgasm ripped through her. Hot and tight, her pussy choked my now-drenched cock and soaked the wand and sheets under her.

What a greedy fucker I turned into, because still I wanted more.

I needed her shivering with the force of my cock pummeling her until the echo of me fucking her pulsed with every step in the days to come. If she rolled over in bed, I wanted the way I carved her up and hollowed her out to be the reason for the groan sliding from her lips.

I wanted her deliciously broken, unable to tackle that mountain, the ache demoting her to the bunny slope.

Over and over, I took her. What started as seductive strokes turned to demands. She fought to stay on the bed and the wand she once straddled and soaked vibrated against my balls and ass.

The tingle began in my spine, the burn spreading under my skin as I fucked her into the mattress with everything I had until tears streamed down her cheeks.

How the fuck could my heart ache so painfully yet burst with such pleasure and possession?

My balls drew up, I gnashed my teeth, and a feral growl tore from my throat as I hammered my release into her.

Her marks burned on my ass with each thrust. She branded my heart with every cry.

Still, I needed more.

Wrapping my fingers around the handle, I popped the plug free from her ass and set off one last climax, leaving her screaming, beating her fists on the bed.

Still pulsing inside her, I turned off the wand, curled over her back, and smoothed away the hair clinging to the side of her face.

My breath caught at the picture she made as

laughter bubbled from her throat. Tears splotched her red cheeks. She glanced at me from the corner of her eye. "You definitely lost your halo tonight," she said with a rasp, making me wonder if I'd hurt her.

Not that she minded, considering I pushed her, and she not only met my demands but toed past the line even farther.

I brushed my knuckles over her cheek. Her eyes sank shut and she curled into my touch. "I only ever had the one you gave me, so I guess it's only fitting that I gave it up for you," I said quietly.

Staring down at her, unable to look away from the exquisitely demolished mess she made, it all became stunningly clear for the first time.

I loved her. Not as a sister. Not as a friend.

But as the one. The only one.

I'd spend the rest of my life wondering when it started and how long I denied the truth of it. But for now, I wanted nothing more than to embrace the revelation settling inside me.

Exhaustion swept in, swift and heavy if the slump of her shoulders was any indication. I scooped her up and settled her under the covers to keep her warm.

The toys went to the tub where I'd clean them up later and the wrecked condom in the trash. Never in my life had I experienced such a beautiful mess.

Before crawling in next to her, I grabbed a couple of waters and snagged a bottle of ibuprofen from my bag.

The minute I raised my arm, she burrowed in beside me and sighed.

"Does it hurt?" I asked as I ran my fingers along her throat.

Her hand drifted over my abs before wrapping around my thickening cock. "Not enough to stop me from doing it all over again."

"You won't be happy until you can't walk or speak, will you?"

"Or maybe I want to get my fill before it's all over."

"Don't piss me off, spawn," I growled the words against her neck as I pulled her over me so she was straddling my hips.

"Listen, it's not my fault the clock is ticking." There it was again. That look of doubt. Vulnerability in the way her eyes landed everywhere except on mine.

I dragged her mouth down and relished the excited squeak she let out as I sucked her tongue into my mouth and smiled. "Fuck the clock. I know where you live."

Breaking the kiss, she sat up, a look of confusion swirling in her eyes. "Funny?"

Tracing the tip of my finger between her breasts, I took in her rosy skin. "I'm not kidding." Waves tumbled over her shoulders and down her arms. I toyed with the ends, unable to tear my gaze away from her.

God, the sight of her stripped bare undid me. No makeup. Just a warm glow and flushed skin. My lungs squeezed. "How did I not see just how stunning you are? God, woman, I wish I could show you what I see when I look at you."

She swallowed hard, her eyes wide. "Nick," she

breathed, the lump in her throat visible with her swallow.

This right here was why I'd needed to memorialize the very second I fell the rest of the way for Charlie McAllister.

Whatever she wanted to say, she could do it later. Right now, I wanted one more taste of that sweet mouth.

One taste and my eyes rolled back in my head.

I glanced over the cell she hadn't noticed in my hand. With a flick of my thumb, I brought up the picture I'd just snagged while I kissed her to make sure I didn't get too much in the image. I was definitely taking a fist to the mouth when Chance got home, but if I sent him a picture of his baby sister's tits, he'd stop my heart, and rightfully so.

My fingers intimately wound in her hair, my fist tight, our mouths slightly open with a definite subtle glimpse of tongue. Charlie looked well and thoroughly fucked.

I grinned, attached the image to the message thread from Chance, and hit send.

"Oh my God! What did you do?"

"Just defining our relationship status."

"But we're not—"

"We are," I said quietly. Tossing my phone on the bedside table, I caught her throat firmly and held her still before me, my thumb stroking back and forth over supple skin. She hovered over me warm and soft, with a lazy smile on her face. A look I planned on seeing every day for an incredibly long while. "I showed up Friday planning to tolerate you. I'm leaving fully planning to have you drive me out of my mind all day, every day, for a lifetime. This doesn't end here, Charlie. It's only the beginning."

EPILOGUE
Charlie

We hadn't gone a single day without seeing each other in the whole next year. Even if it was just an hour to eat dinner together, no matter how busy, we made the time.

Tomorrow we'd head to the lodge for the annual ski trip, our first one since *the* one. Mrs. Mc—er, Ellen—made reservations for cocktails, just between us girls. Calling her by her first name was going to take some getting used to.

She wanted to celebrate my opening my own private office in Galloway Bay. Surprising since the little coastal town where Eve lived was in the opposite direction and a good hour from his parents. It was only a matter of time until we ended up there permanently, and together, but she didn't have to know that just yet.

Baby steps.

As long she didn't poison me at lunch, and she left the grenades at home, I'd be on my best behavior.

We all knew what that meant. I would almost certainly blurt out something terrible that had Ellen tapping into the Urban Dictionary—her new favorite pastime.

I was pretty sure Nick and me falling for each other broke her completely. Watching our moms tiptoe around each other for the first three months of our relationship made my heart ache, wondering if they'd ever find that easy way about them again. They did, but not before our relationship and the harsh words between two best friends threatened to ruin everything.

A week after our ski trip, my mom came by unexpectedly and apologized for the way she treated me. Before she could even get the words out, she dissolved into a puddle of tears. I handled it like a boss, though. I tossed her a box of tissues, prayed she would run dry soon, and poured us both a strong drink.

This was only the beginning… her relationship with Eve was even more strained than hours and in a totally different way. I caved with her first apology, but Eve? The damage was way more significant and I couldn't do one damn thing to help them along.

But I held out hope… and supported them both as best as I could.

Nick never told me the entirety of the conversation he had with our moms that night, but after a glass of whiskey, my mom did. And she cried some more. She'd only just recently started looking him in the eye again and as much as I loved him for standing up for me, for us, I needed us to get back to something normal. I might have given the man some serious hell over the years, but those were just games. Seeing him hurting and disillusioned about his mom, that hit me in every soft spot I never knew I had.

Luckily, we'd all be at the lodge this year. Eve and her girlfriend broke up so she wanted to hightail it out of town for a while, even if that meant spending it with our family.

Chance managed to get leave from the Army and was headed to the airport now to pick up Holly and head up to the lodge a night early. This way Holly and Chance could get some alone time to catch up with our parents before the chaos began since it had been so long since they'd been home for Christmas.

Headlights cut across the living room window and my stomach jumped. Yeah, my stomach still did that a year later, but I sure as hell wasn't telling him. It would go straight to his head and the halo was hard enough to squeeze through the door most days.

Peeling the blinds apart, I spotted him through the window, throwing a grocery bag over his forearm and snagging a duffel from the back seat.

He kept the beard. He said he'd go full-on ZZ Top with it if that's what kept me riding his face.

No shaded to the sharp dressed men, but no.

Besides, I'd developed an addiction to shaving him. A year later and we finally almost made it through a whole shave without him fucking the life out of me on the counter.

He knocked twice and let himself right on in.

The duffel hit the floor. The grocery bag followed.

"Well h—" My words died the minute his hand

wrapped around my throat and he slanted his mouth over mine.

One. Two. Three steps and thunk.

His hot tongue met mine stroke for stroke, sparking fire in my blood. When he bit my lip, I sighed, and he laughed with victory, knowing full well our streak of not getting out a full greeting before we rubbed together like a couple of bitches in heat remained intact.

"You were saying," he murmured over my lips.

"You know, Saint Nick… one of these days we're going to have to learn some restraint. The PTA might frown upon live foreplay demonstrations."

"The PTA, huh?" he said with laughter in his voice. He dragged the tip of his nose over my cheekbone. His fingers flexed on my neck, turning my head just enough to give him access to the soft spot under my jaw he loved so much. "You want me to put a baby in you?"

My thighs clenched. I felt every word of his question throb between my legs and despite how basic it made me, Jesus fuck, when he said it like that? Yeah, I wanted him to put a baby in me. Like yesterday.

His beard scraped along my neck leaving a delicious tingle in its wake. I locked my knees to keep them from giving out. "Will you still love me if I go full-on traditional and say yes?"

"I've loved you through ghost pepper sauce and your Charlie Scissorhands era, so yeah," he grinned nipping my chin. "A little traditional breeding kink Charlie can't scare me."

I wound my arms around his neck and stretched in his arms like a cat. "You've loved me that long, huh?"

"I'm pretty sure, but don't tell your brother. He's finally come to terms with this. The last thing I need is for him to question every time we've been together since forever. I already have a full-time job." He cupped my jaw and tipped my face up to his. God the height on this man had me all sorts of hot and bothered. "Besides, the halo kept the dirty thoughts at bay. My heart though, he was all in. He just waited a while before he let me in on the secret."

My cell pinged at the same time his vibrated. Breaking apart, we both checked our phones.

"It's Holly." His brows snapped together. "She said the storm is already hitting and they've only made it to Freeport."

"Chance sent a voice message. Hang on."

I cranked up the volume and hit play. "I'm giving this twenty more minutes and if we don't get ahead of this storm, we're going to hole up somewhere until the it passes. I'll keep you posted. Mom's going to be pissed."

"Mom's going to be pissed?" Nick said as he tapped out a message to Holly, his thumbs getting more aggressive with every letter. "I've got news for him; he's got a hell of a lot more to be worried about than your mother if he gets a room with my sister."

I bit back the laugh, kinda. It came out as more of a snort. Fitting all things considered. "What are you gonna do, tell him not to fuck your baby sister?"

The man dead-ass looked me straight in the eye. "You're damn right, I am!"

Oh, look at him all full of righteous indignation. "Hey, Nick?"

He jammed a hand through his hair, pacing as he stared down at the phone. "What?"

"How did that work when Chance said it to you?"

Nick skidded to a stop and snarled, actually snarled at me. "I fucked his baby sister."

"And fucked her so damn good." The laugh finally broke free. "With toys," I pointed out.

Nick's phone vibrated again and his heated gaze shot straight to the screen. I'd never heard the sound that came out of him next. A whimper mixed with a hiss. Nah, that wasn't it. Whatever it was, it was animalistic and had me peering down at the screen next to him.

HOLLY

We passed three cars that slid off the road in the past two miles. Chance called it. We're getting a room.

NICK

You better mean two rooms.

HOLLY

Great in theory, but unfortunately, a lot of people had the same idea. They've only got one room left.

"Oh no… no. No. No!" He added a stomp to his

pace and instead of shoving his hand through his hair this time, he all but yanked it making it stand up on end.

Not going to lie, it looked way sexier when I did it.

"Nick…" I laid my palm on his chest where his racing heart threatened to jump clean out of his body. "It's fine… they never liked each other, anyway. Nothing's going to happen in one night."

"We didn't like each other either and on the first night, I kissed you, fed you, and called you a 'good girl.'"

I wrapped my hands around his forearm and smiled up at him, enjoying the turbulence rolling off him. I knew just how to put that to good use. "Yeah, but you're an overachiever. Chance is not you."

CHANCE

Got a room with Holly, but don't worry, I'll honor the code, bro. The same way you did.

NICK

Do not fuck my baby sister.

CHANCE

Cross my heart.

NICK

Hope to die, stick a needle in my eye… I'll drive railroad spikes through your eye sockets if you touch her.

CHANCE

I just took her suitcase from her. Our hands mighta brushed a little.

NICK

Not funny.

CHANCE

Neither was the picture you sent right after you fucked Charlie's brains out for the first time. I practically saw my baby sister's O-face man. You ever see Holly's O-face???

NICK

Chaaaaannnnnnnccccccceeeeee!

CHANCE

Niiiiiiicccccccckkkkkkkk?

My phone vibrated, and I glanced down at the screen abandoning the pissing contest between my brother and Nick.

HOLLY

Mayday… don't show my brother, he'll lose it. But Charlie, there's only one bed.

Welp, that's something.

I glanced up at Nick and found him slack-jawed, reading his sister's message.

Nick tipped his head up at the ceiling, closed his eyes, and pinched the bridge of his nose. "This cannot be happening."

HOLLY

Also, when did your brother get this hot?

Oh shit.

I locked the screen as fast as I could, fumbling the phone before catching it. With as much chill as I could muster, I slid it in my back pocket. "So… Nick, why don't we exchange presents now? What do you say?"

A vein throbbed in his forehead. Huh, that was new. "What did she say?"

I waved away his question. "Nothing major. It's fine. Everything is fine."

"That's what everyone says when it's not fine, Charlie." Red splotches formed on his cheeks.

Taking his hand, I hauled him over to the couch. "They're adults. It's one night. Whatever's going to happen is going to happen. In the meantime, though, I've got something special for ya."

He dropped onto the couch, his head lolling back with a sigh. "I hope it's an escape plan for when I kill your brother?"

"Cute, but nope, this one is sooooo much better. Here." Dropping onto the floor on the other side of the coffee table in front of my small, but festive as fuck tree, I grabbed the present I'd been jonesing to give him. The idea came to me shortly after we got back from last year's ski trip. For someone like me, that's an agonizing length of time to wait. But I had to wait until I knew for sure this thing between us was going to be *the thing*—you know, of the rest of our lives variety, forever kind of thing.

I handed him a shiny red gift bag with metallic gold paper spilling out and sat back on my heels knowing we were about to make a memory we'd be telling our kids, and their kids for years to come.

He peered into the bag, narrowed his eyes, and glanced up at me. "It doesn't bite, right?"

"Nope."

Piece by piece he pulled out stuffing until comical confusion crossed his face.

"What the hell…" he trailed off, pulling each out, one hook at a time, and lining them up on the table between us. He held the stuffed, blue jean ball up between us, trying to make out what he was looking at. Then he grabbed the white one, followed by the red one made out of the same material as what used to be his favorite basketball shorts.

"You. Little. Shit." He grinned and threw the white ball ornament at me. "You made Christmas ornaments out of my crotches."

Ducking fast, the ornament sailed right over my head straight at the tree. The hook snagged on a branch and the crotch of his tighty whitey underwear swung back and forth until they settled, blending in with the rest of the ornaments.

Flushed with laughter, bracing my hands on the carpet so I didn't fall over, I managed to squeak out a reply. "A whole set."

"Charlie…" Leaning over, he settled his palms on the coffee table as though he was ready to launch right over it and grab me. With a hot gleam in his eye, he said. "You better run."

BONUS
Short Story

NICK

Chance's ass better show up.

After all, the bastard evened the score.

Or he had until I knocked his sister up.

My gaze landed on where Charlie stood next to *her* wishing tree. Yeah, that's she had started calling it—with typical Charlie emphasis—after I matched her donation for the first time two years ago. The little demon did everything possible to make it abundantly clear she'd staked her claim on it, including stomping her foot Charlie style with an exasperated, "I saw it first!"

Yeah, well she could bite me. The little shit.

Every few seconds she'd sneak a peek at those little angel skirts with that devious look in her eye. She totally planned to get the jump on me, but I had news for her, this year would be different. I'd already made the arrangements. If she was a good girl, maybe I'd let her in on them.

I spotted my mother headed Charlie's way and instinctually held my breath, my jaw tight. While she'd made huge strides in accepting Charlie, I still didn't trust her, not completely. There was something soul-crushing about seeing someone you considered your hero turn into someone you didn't recognize and couldn't count on. Charlie had a lot of years of hurt with her mom she'd been used to where I'd had no such history with my own mother. Getting over it would take me a minute.

We'd get there.

My phone vibrated, and my screen lit up with a text from Chance.

About damn time.

CHANCE

Headed in. You better have my whiskey waiting, ya fucker.

ME

Aren't you a moody bitch?

CHANCE

And remember, no eye contact.

ME

Yes, my delicate little petal.

CHANCE

Bite me.

ME

Can't. When I bite, I do it with eye contact. Just ask your sister.

CHANCE

FML

And that's what the son of a bitch got for keeping

me waiting for a good twenty minutes at the damn bar when I could have been across the room with my hands on Charlie.

Craning my neck, I shifted over a couple of feet until I could see the exchange more clearly.

My mother leaned in and kissed Charlie's cheek, but Charlie did her one better and wrapped her arms around my mother in a warm hug.

Well, fuck me.

Goddamn the woman. There were days she pushed me right to the absolute edge of my sanity only to have moments like these—sweet and selfless—yanking me back.

I studied the look in my mother's eyes and the smile on her face, and prayed this would be one more good interaction to build back the complete trust I'd once had in her.

As though Charlie could feel my stare, she caught my gaze from across the room and mouthed the words she'd been telling me for the past two years.

Fix your face.

I couldn't stop the grin tipping the corner of my mouth. She looked so warm and soft, with her cheeks flushed, and her hair in a messy knot on top of her head. You'd never know how up to about a week ago, morning sickness had been making her its bitch for the past four months.

You'd also never know she edged the shit out of me before coming down here tonight… payback for my locking down my dick after she had an episode of spotting. Naturally, immediately following the first time I touched her since she'd been plagued with morning sickness.

The midwife said everything was fine, but fuck me, I was not fine.

But with the all clear, determination flared in her eyes once again in that familiar way, leading to a hell of a comeback. Food stayed down, spirits stayed up, and she had an insatiable urge to make up for everything she missed being sick for so long.

And when the hell had Charlie become the chill one? It's like she'd reached some zen little happy zone where she took everything in stride. Okay, so she hadn't taken the way I locked down my dick with stride.

My mother glanced down at Charlie's belly, a look of longing on her face, and that tender-hearted part of Charlie she used to keep wrapped in rusted razor wire immediately recognized what my mother wanted. With one arm still around my mom's shoulder, Charlie took my mother's hand and laid it over our baby.

My heart in my throat and my chest squeezing impossibly tight, I could only stare as Charlie did something I knew to be incredibly difficult for her while making it look effortless.

My ability to take a deep breath fled, and my heartbeat raced right along after it.

Even that was part of her devious plan… making me fall in love with her hundreds times over.

I caught a glimpse of Chance as he stepped into the lodge making his way straight to the bar. Hopping up on the bar stool, I kicked out the one next to me when Chance arrived.

Grabbing the waiting glass, he slid onto the seat, his attention aimed at our families congregating across the room, and nodded in their direction. "How's she feeling?"

"Full." The word popped out before I could stop it. Definitely got that from Charlie.

Chance choked on the whiskey he'd just tipped back and sputtered into a flimsy bar napkin. "Dude. I'm going to need that to never be your fucking answer again."

I bit back my smug grin and shrugged, completely enjoying this new ground we'd reached. Where we talked easily again, and I got to see the soft spot he had for his baby sister in a whole new way. "I gotta level with you. I don't think you'd like my other answer either."

"Yeah, well try me."

I tapped my fingers on the edge of my glass and went in for the kill. "Horny as fuck. I can barely keep up with her."

Chance groaned and pinched the bridge of his nose. "This is my life now, isn't it?"

I'd joke about it until we reached the point where he could shrug this all off. We may have made a ton of progress, but we weren't quite there yet.

"A little bit, but how about this, I'll go easy on you if you just call an end to the no eye contact rule."

The problem was, Chance was my ride-or-die my whole life. He knew my every experience. He knew every woman I'd been with. My best friend for life, we'd definitely talked about our favorite ways to get off a time or two… only now he knew I did all of those things and then some with, and to, his sister.

He turned to me, his gaze pretty much landing on my chin, the chicken. "You know the deal. Six months of no eye contact every time you make me see the aftermath of stuffing my sister."

I nudged him with my elbow. "I haven't sent a picture like that in almost a year."

"No, you just got her pregnant so every time I look at her, I'm reminded you've not only been in her, but you're still in her," he mumbled into his glass.

"You should really see a therapist."

"Maybe, but for tonight, this will do," Chance said, raising his glass, clinking it against mine, and knocking the rest of the amber liquid back. "When do you plan to drop the news that you guys are married?"

My gaze landed on my empty ring finger. "Christmas Eve. It's a combination gift for our mothers." It had only been a week since we snuck off and took the vows, but in those seven days, I'd gotten very used to that ring. So much so that I found myself constantly fiddling with the empty space there.

"The fact that you're married?"

"Nope. The big ceremony. We're giving it to them."

"So basically you're you two are permanently solidifying favorite status," he said followed by a scoff. "Damn. None of us will be able to top that."

"That's right," I said with a laugh. "Charlie never

wanted a big elaborate wedding and frankly, neither did I. So we did it our way and left the big production to them."

Chance let out a long-suffering sigh and stood. "Welp, might as well enjoy my next couple days as the favorite before you strip me of my status. Let's do this."

They huddled with their backs to us now, facing the tall windows overlooking the slopes. Hands flew as they talked, their heads tipping back with laughter. I slid in behind Charlie, my arms going around her, resting my hands over the soft sweater stretching over the gentle swell of her belly.

"You're lucky I love you and recognized you sneaking in. Someone touches this belly, I lash out first and ask questions later."

"Maybe, but there are exceptions." I brushed a kiss over her neck, making her shiver. God, I loved how she couldn't hold that back. "I saw you with my mom."

She snorted. "I'm getting soft."

"I'm starting to realize you always were. You just surrounded that tender heart with Anthrax."

A sigh slipped from her lips, and she settled into my embrace even more. "I miss my Anthrax."

"You're incredibly generous, making yourself uncomfortable so you can share our baby with her."

"It's amazing what I can accomplish when I steal your halo."

"*Borrowed*. I find you slide it off as soon as you're done with it. Afraid you'll get stuck that way, no doubt. An angel wouldn't have left me limping with the most painful hard-on of my life earlier." Just having her in my arms stealing a chance to nuzzle into her soft hair had the lingering tension dissipating.

"Keep torturing me by holding out, and it will only get worse," she said giving my hand a reassuring pat.

"Soon."

"Better be or I'm going to take matters into my own hands."

I spun her in my arms and pressed a soft kiss to her smart mouth. "After how long we've waited, that would just be mean."

"I've reached peak desperation." She ground her fingers into her temple and sighed. "It's every man for himself. Better keep an eye on me Nick. You never know what I'll do."

"Just remember the deal, I get right of first refusal to watch."

"Yes my little fiend," she said smiling up at me.

I searched the room searching for a distraction, just needing her to hold out a bit longer. Tables and chairs had been arranged around the perimeter leaving a huge open section of people congregated in chatty little groups, their second, third, maybe even fourth cocktail in their hands. The lights had dimmed two songs ago and the DJ in the corner had subtly turned up the music. A few couples had started drifting toward the open floor, swaying and smiling.

I nudged her chin with my knuckle, tipping her face up to mine. "Dance with me."

Her eyebrows snapped together forming this little V

right above the bridge of her nose. "What? No." She started shaking her head and shot a hand up between us. "NO."

"Come on?"

"You do remember those swing dance lessons when we were kids, right?"

I dropped a kiss on her forehead. "I do."

Palm to my chest, she gave me a shove. "And you mastered the moves in about a week."

"I did. It helped that the teacher was hot."

"Of course it did," she muttered with laughter in her voice. "And I—"

"Wouldn't put that big dick of yours away long enough to be led. Not even by the other teacher." I nuzzled her neck and laced my fingers with hers. "Come on, spawn. Put your big dick away and dance with me."

The opening beat of Grand Folk Railroad's *Some Kind of Wonderful* kicked up, the kind of song where you could dance in a circle of friends or with a partner. I wanted nothing more than to watch her ivory sweater dress flirt with her thighs through every shift and turn.

Turning her face to mine, she bit down on her bottom lip and it curved in an evil little smile. "You know, Nick. If I have to put it away now, it's only going to come out bigger and badder later. You ready for that?"

"Try me."

She smirked with a secret in those silver eyes "Don't say I didn't warn you."

She was up to something, but I'd suffer whatever it

was for this. With a tug, I spun her into my arms and kissed her plump mouth and almost completely lost myself to the way she nestled into my arms and moved against me.

"Come on." My voice came out gruff and heat flared in her eyes. "Down Charlie. Soon."

"Soon," she huffed. "It's always *soon*."

I led her into the crowd, somewhere a bit more inconspicuous until I could loosen her up, and took her hands. "Three steps forward, light on the third, then three back, remember."

"Yeah, yeah, yeah," she muttered as she shuffled into position while staring down at our feet.

"Then follow the line."

"Got it," she said with a forced confidence I knew she didn't feel.

"And Charlie, pay attention to the tension in my hand and wrist and where it's leading you."

"See, it's that part there my brain really hates."

"No doubt."

We eased into the steps, just the three forward, three back, and my guiding her down the line until we switched sides. I didn't lead right off the bat because even though she agreed to put that figurative cock of her in a cage, there was no way she could resist smacking me right in the mouth with it if I came in too hot too soon.

With just a few switch-ups, she'd finally stopped sneaking glances at the people around us to see if they were watching. On the fourth, I led her into a twirl right under my arm that had her throwing her head back, her breathless laugh mingling with the sound of the music.

She glowed from head to toe and the sweater dress didn't disappoint. The belt tied gently just over the swell of our baby captured my gaze every time. But it was the flashes of soft, thick thighs as the ribbing of the dress crept up and shifted that had me hard enough to pound nails.

Jesus Christ. This woman was going to be the death of me, but what a way to go.

She gave me one defiance-free dance and instead of pushing my luck, I wrapped her in my arms and swayed with her on the floor, taking in every inch of the smiling face tipped up to mine.

"Thank you," I said quietly, the unplanned words surprising me.

"For what?"

"For not taking no for an answer. For pushing every boundary. For trusting me with the parts you had every reason to hide." Forehead pressed to hers, I hovered over her lips and let her heat seep into me. "For turning my entire life upside down and making it better than I ever knew it could be."

Her lips parted on a wobbly breath. Tears rose fast and furious in her eyes and one hot tear blazed a damp trail down her cheek. "Always a smooth fucker."

Compliments still made her uneasy. They healed, but they hurt too. They shone a spotlight on her she couldn't quite embrace, but she'd gotten better about it. That was the best part of moments like these. They pushed her, but they were private. In this cocoon between us, she didn't hide from them.

I brushed away the lock of hair clinging to her damp cheek. "And for cutting the crotches out of all of my underwear, shorts, and jeans."

A laugh bubbled up from her throat washing away the tears. Her forehead fell against my chest as she dissolved into a fit of watery giggles.

"But Charlie, the ghost pepper stunt is still bullshit."

Rocking with her in my arms, I grinned over the top of her head and caught Chance watching us, an easy smile on his face. His eyes flicked up to mine.

Busted, asshole.

His gaze slid away with a grimace as he strategically scratched his jaw with a middle finger aimed right at me.

2
Charlie

Nick was up to something. I knew it. I'd been waiting for him to call it a night for over two hours, but nope, he showed no sign of tiring.

Well, if I had any hope of making it through all the shopping I had to do tomorrow for the angels, I needed rest.

And an orgasm.

Okay, at least three. He better give me *at least* three. The first one would be easy. I swear, all he had to do was look my clit right in the eye, and she'd succumb to his every charm and flutter at his feet.

He owed me dammit. Strutting around all cocky and shit still reveling in the knowledge he'd knocked me up with his baby. Anyone else would look like a pompous asshole doing that, but not Nick. Never Nick.

He looked like a damn God.

The bastard knew it, too.

By day, he moved through his career all unassuming-like. A financial planning wizard for clients he genuinely liked and cared about. Then, taking those same tools he used helping modest families, he created highly uncon-

209

ventional strategies on a corporate level with select high-profile clients he'd accepted so he could increase his pro bono work. A natural philanthropist to the core.

By night, he puffed right up with pride, his ego practically needing to be greased up to stuff it through the doorways.

At the moment, as he chatted with a cluster of our parents' friends, flashing me a toe-curling smile, he was a stunning combo of the two.

What the hell was he waiting for? I know he needed the damn orgasm as much as I did at this point. I made sure of it.

Plus, I had everything in the works to make sure the very next orgasm he had would be the most mind-blowing of his life.

If. He'd. Stop. Talking.

Most of the crowd celebrating tonight had called it a night, with just a few diehards clinging to every last minute they could squeeze out.

Thankfully the DJ switched to the low hum of instrumental music and they turned up the lights a bit, signaling the end. Sinking into a plush chair in the corner, I drew up my feet underneath me and settled in to wait. I folded my hands on the padded arm of the chair and laid my head down.

I'd just rest. For only a minute.

I felt the smallest kick in my belly and smiled, my eyes drifting shut.

"Hey, wake up… I have a surprise for you."

"Hmmmm, orgasms?" I leaned into Nick's warm palm along my cheek, but didn't open my eyes. If anything, I snuggled deeper into the chair.

"Soon," he said with a laugh.

My eyes popped open then, and I gave him a glare that even the weight of sleep couldn't conceal. "That is my new most-hated word."

His eyes danced. They laughed at my horny misery. "I have an early Christmas present."

"Me too… and if you'd stop saying *soon*, I could give it to you."

"It'll be worth the wait, I promise."

"What time is it?" I sat up and stretched as I glanced around the room. The only people left were the staff cleaning up and the maintenance guy, John, who'd worked at the lodge for as long as I could remember. He stood by the tree, his forearms propped on a rung of a massive ladder.

"Just after midnight." He crouched in front of me, took my hands, and made lazy circles with his thumb over my knuckles.

"How long was I sleeping?"

"A little over an hour." Pushing to his feet, he drew me up and settled his hand along my hip to steady me.

It's amazing how something inside you the size of an ear of corn could have you so off balance.

"Long enough for everyone to clear out so we could have some privacy. Come on," he said, leading me over to the tree where John smiled and opened a huge trash bag.

"We ready to do this, kids?"

I glanced between the two of them, just a tad irritated that there was a plan for *my* tree, but I was the only one who didn't know about it. "What are we doing?"

"We're taking all of them."

"We—wait, what?"

He rocked back on his heels practically dancing on the balls of his feet. "A clean sweep."

"Nick, that has to be…" My gut bottomed as I thought about the small dent my five thousand dollars worth two years ago looked versus the tree full of angels as a whole. "I don't even want to say the number."

His eyes roamed the tree from the bottom to the top. "Best guess, about a hundred thousand."

Okay, I was definitely still sleeping. I pinched my arm making sure to dig in the nails good and hard. It fucking hurt. "So, did I miss a redwood-sized money tree sprouting from your ass?"

"Nope, I just didn't tell you about the hefty bonus I got from CoreShield about a month ago."

"How much are we talking? You still have taxes to pay on that?"

"I do, but they were so impressed with the work I did that when I told them what I planned to do with the bonus, they said they'd match it. We can wipe the tree clean this year." He grinned down at me. "The best part is, no one will know who did it, but everyone will be talking about it. The mystery turning into a legend just might be enough to get people participating in it for years to come."

"Permanent halo status, Nick?" My eyes prickled again and a heavy heat spread through my chest. He knew I struggled with walking away from this tree each year and he undoubtedly knew this year would hit even harder. Hormones.

And did he just have a solution for this year? Of course not. If anyone would figure out a way to make it pay off for years to come, it was my husband.

"Yeah, but now we'll have a matching pair."

"What about all the shopping?" Was there even enough time to pull that off between the two of us?

"I worked out help for that too. Ready to strip that tree?" He brushed a knuckle over my belly. Before he could drop his hand, I snagged it in my own.

A spurt of energy coursed through me, spiking my blood. "Let's do it."

He let me help for all of twenty minutes until they were too high up to reach. The minute I stepped one foot on the ladder, he was there, snatching me right back. "I don't think so."

I swatted his hands away. Not that it deterred him. "Pregnant, not broken."

"But tired and more off balance than normal. No."

"It was one step."

"With you, it's never just one anything. We've got this. Relax. You can supervise."

I called all the bullshit on his promoting me to supervisor. He meant *watch*.

213

With a smile, which should have been his first clue, I took a step back. I nodded and smiled every time they glanced in my direction. All agreeable and shit while I had to be, but the minute they were distracted with the last of the angels, I headed for our room.

He really thought he could placate me that easily? Nope. Not a chance. So, instead, I would make use of the renewed energy and stubborn resolve thanks to my nap and glowing personality and... *play*.

I'd show him supervise.

After peeling off my knee-high boots, I grabbed the cloth bag I'd slipped in my suitcase when he wasn't looking. And in it—what was called the Rolls Royce of clit vibrators. At least it better be at almost two hundred dollars.

If he didn't hurry up, he'd miss the show because I was done waiting. I left my hair up, he loved taking it down too much for me to steal that from him. With the comforter peeled back and the packaging discarded, I set the plastic fob on the nightstand and climbed onto the bed—dead center—and settled against the pillows.

All the pillows.

Like a fucking queen. He wanted to pamper me. Fine. I'd get on board.

We were in the same room. The one we'd gotten stuck in two years ago. The one we always came back to now. I took in the couch, the mini bar, and the door where my toy arsenal hung and smiled. Making a deal with a saint turned out to be the smartest thing I'd ever done.

Memories, one after another, cascaded through my mind. Watching him sleep, shaving him for the first time, and there, right next to the bed, the wall where he kissed me when he found out about my secret with the angels. Kissed me so deeply, he practically flicked my clit from the inside out.

My heart raced even now, my skin growing hot and tight. This was a damn good room.

I had just turned on the toy when he barged in, all fired up. "I swear I'm going to break this habit you have of up and disappearing on me."

I shrugged a shoulder. "You didn't want my help. You relegated me to watching. I'm not the voyeur, Nick. You are."

"I didn't want you on the ladder."

I directed my attention to the toy and turned it over in my hand. "That's how I help."

"Chaaarrrrrrlllllliiiiiiieeeee," he growled.

"Niiiccccccckkkkkkk." I brushed my thumb over the curved oval opening checking for sharp edges or any imperfections. "You had one job, Nicky boy. My orgasms. You missed the deadline so I had to take matters into my own hands."

"I've got two commercial-sized bags of angels I had to haul up here and you're playing?"

I let my legs fall open giving him a glimpse of just how ready to play I was.

"Little shit," he mumbled from the foot of the bed as he yanked the ends of his dress shirt out of his pants and started working on the buttons. "Tell me you had on underwear downstairs."

"Nope."

When I reached for the hem of my dress, he shot me a glare. "Don't you dare take it off."

"Nick, it's *soon*. You will give me my orgasms or I'm going to bite you."

"I will, but revealing those gorgeous thighs is my job. I've been dreaming about it since the first moment I saw you in that dress."

I nudged the knit band up just enough to settle the smooth end of the vibrator against my clit, the sensation, a vibration, but also this slight movement of air that had the gasp sputtering in my throat. Oh God, this thing was good. So good.

His sense of urgency increased and with it, his clumsiness as he fought to stay upright with each piece of clothing he struggled to shed.

The change in my breathing with the low hum of the toy filled the quiet of the room. Nick's heated gaze stayed transfixed on my hand.

Wet, swollen, and absolutely dying for release, I stretched out and increased the pressure, my arm tossed over my head, as I writhed there, my fingers fisting the pillow behind me.

"Fuck." He kicked his pants free of his feet and dove for me, his hands wrapping around my knees as he settled between my legs. Mesmerized in a way I hadn't seen in months, he devoured every last bit of the show.

The way I brought myself to the brink, but yanked

myself back, time and time again, knowing when I finally let go, every cell in my body would explode with it. I relished the little gasps bursting from his lips every time he anticipated my toppling over.

What an equal opportunity edger I was.

By the third time though, he lost every bit of restraint and covered my hand with his. "Do it!" he commanded, as he kissed the inside of my thigh. The pressure he applied sealed the gap between the toy and my aching clit which heightened the sensation tenfold.

"Bossy fucker," I choked out as I rocked into the force of our hands working in unison.

"I'll make it up to you," he said, his gravelly voice vibrating along my skin.

Burying my fingers in his hair, I finally let go, the hot flow of release coursing through with every rock of my hips. Pleasure bordering the point of pain pulsed, and I cried out. Too much and not enough, I lay there at the mercy of my body.

And because he knew me—all of me—every last part I never wanted to show anyone, he knew just what to do to keep my pleasure suspended. He yanked the toy away and sent it flying to the foot of the bed. Grasping the edges of my dress with his balled fists, he shoved the knit clean up to my hips, and dove in with his demanding, wicked fucking mouth.

My vision blurred with the first swipe of his tongue. Goosebumps bloomed on my skin the minute he sucked my clit between his lips. But it was that hum of satisfaction vibrating as he ate that had a ragged groan tearing through me while I writhed under the assault of his skilled mouth.

I became absolutely feral listening to him devour me, savoring the satisfied sounds rumbling from his throat. Loving the possessive way his arms locked me in place so there was nowhere to escape. I gave into every sensation wracking my body until the tension snapped and my back arched with wave after wave of pure bliss.

The buzzing in my head obliterated his murmured words as I collapsed bonelessly against the pile of pillows behind me.

I barely noticed the dress disappearing over my head but sighed with relief when my hair tumbled free under his deft fingers. His scent surrounded me, driving me mad with the deep spicy notes in his cologne.

Before I could so much as clear my vision, he splayed my legs wide. Kneeling before me, his mouth devouring mine, the taste of us, of what he did to me with every touch only added fuel to the fire.

"I didn't think it was possible to want you more, but damn woman." He bit my lip and soothed the sting with his hot tongue. "You are so damn responsive. I'm absolutely savage watching you fall apart."

Wrapping my arms around his neck, a sense of peace filled me as I clung to him, not realizing how much I needed this with him again. Morning sickness gave zero fucks about normal work hours, sleep cycles, or needing to be close to your person. For the last few months we'd been at its mercy, but we were totally going to make up for it now.

I smiled against his neck while he continued to stroke his hands along my spine. Even though I savored every single pass, I also had other plans.

His present.

"Hey, Nick…"

"Hmmm?" he hummed as he trailed his lips along my jaw.

"Remember the big dick you had me put away before…"

He stilled but didn't pull away. "What about it?"

"It's bigger."

"Okaaaay?"

"And badder."

A laughed rumbled in his chest. "I'm listening."

"Go get your present… blue bag on the table."

He managed to snag the pouch without losing that possessive grip he had on me leg.

Always with the hands on me, not that I was complaining. Secretly, I loved the hell out of it.

Unzipping the three sides, he flipped the top back and pulled the other toy out of the bag.

Cocking his head, he took in the slopes and curves. "It's high quality, I'll give you that, but I'm surprised. Seems a little tame for you."

Oh this was going to be good. "It's not for me."

He turned it over in his hand and glanced up at me. "Huh?"

"It doesn't go inside me."

He scratched the edge of his jaw and shook his head. "I don't understand."

"It goes inside *you*."

"Inside of wh—" His hands shot up between us. *"Wait!"*

"As I recall, your words were, 'Try me.'"

"Yes, but—"

Not so cool anymore was he? I dragged my fingers over my nipple drawing his gaze. When I had his attention again, I raised an eyebrow. "Scared?"

He stared at my breasts longingly and swallowed hard. "Terrified. It looks like a lot."

God, I loved when he was helpless to look away from me. "You just got done calling it tame."

"That was before I knew where you wanted to put it."

"Baby, you aren't going to want to fuck me without that once you get a taste of what it does." Pushing up onto my knees, I brushed my lips over his reassuringly as I stroke my fingertips over the soft beard I loved so damn much. "If you want to stop, we stop."

Peppering soft kisses on the underside of his jaw, I glided my palms over his ribs, stroking every sexy dip. God, I'd never get sick of touching this man, tasting him, and pushing him in ways he never imagined.

With every soft stroke he relaxed a fraction more. The air grew hotter between us and the apprehension radiating from him turned to surrender.

"I'm going to hold you to that," he said as he tossed the vibrator on the bed. Clasping my chin, he stole a hard, hot kiss from my mouth.

"Lay down."

With one final burning glance, he sprawled over the mattress on his stomach. Folding his hands under his head, he watched my every move. He tried to hide it, but the click of the lube cap flipping open made him jump.

Crawling over his calves, I settled between his knees, nudging them apart. Starting with the toy, I coated the silicone and then squeezed out a generous amount on my fingers.

"You know I'm going to own you after this, right? You're going to do everything I want. When I want." Relishing this new, heady sense of power, I spanked him and palmed the muscle after, enjoying what had to be the most phenomenal ass I'd ever seen.

"You're putting a whole lot of faith in one simple toy," he said with heated challenge in his eyes as he aimed a look over his shoulder.

Holding eye contact, I streaked the lube right between his cheeks. The minute I hit his asshole, his jaw went slack and his eyes glazed over.

"Fuck," he breathed, his eyelids sliding shut.

Victory.

"I see I've got your attention."

His eyes cracked open, his heavy-lidded stare on me. "All of my attention."

I glided the tip of the curved prostate massager along the same trail I made with the lube. With a few gentle adjustments that had him sinking his teeth into his bottom lip, I carefully worked it in.

His body reacted in a multitude of ways. First with

resistance, until I lovingly bit his ass cheek to distract him.

A third of the way in, his shoulders and back muscles rolled and flexed as a groan slid from his parted lips.

Two-thirds of the way in, his toes curled, and he dug his fists into the mattress with a few rapid pants.

But when it slid in the rest of the way and settled into place, the base nestling right along his taint, and resting gently against the back of his balls, a shudder moved through him that had me positively trembling with him.

His back arched ever so slowly, his jaw clenched, and when he turned his gaze back to me, his dark eyes became laser-focused on me like I was his fucking prey.

Pushing onto his knees, his chest heaved as he absorbed this new, unfamiliar, but judging by the flush crawling over his skin, wild sensation filling him. "You are the Devil. Fuck."

I crawled up next to him, kneaded his fine ass cheek once more while I kissed him slow and deep. Sucking his tongue into my mouth, I gave him no way to retreat.

His fingers shot out locking on the back of my neck and before I even got my bearings, he dragged me under him, splayed my legs wide, and plunged in deep and hard.

My mouth fell open on a wheeze and my eyes rolled back. Fuck yes.

Finally out of his own head, he stopped treating me

like a piece of porcelain and took. Thank fuck, he finally took.

With a grunt, he closed his eyes and hung his head, his lungs heaving. "Sorceress," he muttered with a hiss as he flexed his hips.

And now that I had him where I wanted him, I had every intention of keeping him there. Completely at my mercy.

"You have no idea." Walking my hand along the nightstand, my fingertips landed right on the fob, and I pressed the button.

His eyes shot open and glazed over.

My breath caught in my throat and a smile of pure triumph spread over my face as he went absolutely insane above me.

"It's everywhere," he ground out. "Jesus, I feel everything. Inside and out," he said last with a choked groan.

Finesse went completely out the window. He buried his face between my breasts as he fisted my hair. Holding me immobilized, he fed off my body.

The simplest touch of his lips on my nipples had me levitating these days. But tonight, the way he devoured my flesh in this perfect storm of crude sucking, biting, and licking left me stunned, helpless to whatever he delivered next.

And oh, did he deliver.

With his free hand locked on my hip, he pounded into me hard and fast, the orgasm coming in so swift, so intense, the ability to scream locked tight in my throat as I stared up into his blazing eyes.

Just as the waves began to ebb, he dragged out of me completely, his thumb going straight to my clit, making it impossible to come down. With his other hand, he plunged his fingers into me fast and steady.

His demanding gaze locked on the absolute destruction he sought between my thighs, and in seconds, I was whimpering helplessly. The flood he demanded from me rose swiftly and soaked the bed earning a growl of triumph from deep in his chest.

"Fuck, that's beautiful. Goddamn." His hand settling over my jaw, he took my mouth deep and hard, mirroring the complete domination with his hips and cock. His lungs heaved, his breaths going from deep and rhythmic to jagged and sporadic. With each deliciously violent crash of his hips, he panted every crazed sensation coursing through him into my lungs.

On his last thrust, he punched his fist into the pillows on either side of my head, his shoulders locking. His spine locked so tight, he seemed as though he would snap at the slightest pressure. The booming shout of pleasure or agony, my God who knew with the way his teeth ground together, echoed through him.

I cupped his jaw and stroked my thumb over his beard as he struggled for air. Beads of sweat welled up on the ridges of his shoulders, over this chest, along his temples, and along the edges of his hair.

A rapt fascination overtook me as I watched the bead of moisture breaking free along his neck right before trailing down into the hair on his chest.

With a last burst of energy, I pushed up just enough to lick the salt from his skin.

He hissed and his eyes flashed.

All. Fucking. Mine.

Staying firmly buried inside me, he spent the next several minutes coming down under the soothing glide of my hands roaming his skin. With his forehead propped on the pillow next to me, he kept his back arched, keeping his weight off of me and the baby.

Controlled madness.

He turned to me and dropped a series of gentle kisses along my jaw all the way to the soft skin under my ear. "Tell me I didn't hurt you."

"You didn't hurt me."

"Promise me you're not lying."

"Cross my heart."

He pushed up on his fists and stared down at me, his eyes searching mine. "You own my ass now."

I sputtered out a laugh at the incredulous tone of his voice and did my best not to gloat. "It's all mine. I bet you'll never ask me to put my dick away again, will you?"

for all things echo...

For new books, old books, tastes-great-less-filling books,
signings, playlists, story boards, and so much more,
go to my website.

www.EchoGrayce.com

And for the latest news, and let's face it, all the
announcements I will absolutely forget to put on social
media, sign up for my newsletter while you're there!